Carleton Renaissance Plays

D0509702

General Editors: Donald Beecher, Massimo Ciavolella

Editorial Advisors: Douglas Campbell (Carleton), Peter Clive (Carleton), Louise George Clubb (Berkeley), Bruno Damiani (Catholic University of America), Louise Fothergill-Payne (Calgary), Peter Fothergill-Payne (Calgary), Amilcare Iannucci (Toronto), Jean-Marie Maguin (Montpellier), Domenico Pietropaolo (Toronto), Anthony Raspa (Chicoutimi), Leonard Sbrocchi (Ottawa), Pamela Stewart (McGill).

Carleton Renaissance Plays in Translation offer the student, scholar, and general reader a selection of sixteenth-century masterpieces in modern English translations, most of them for the first time. The texts have been chosen for their intrinsic merits and for their importance in the history of the development of the theatre. Each volume contains a critical and interpretative introduction intended to increase the enjoyment and understanding of the text. Reading notes illuminate particular references, allusions, and topical details. The comedies chosen as the first texts have fast-moving plots filled with intrigues. The characters, though cast in the stock patterns of the genre, are witty and amusing portraits reflecting Renaissance social customs and pretensions. Not only are these plays among the most celebrated of their own epoch, but they directly influenced the development of comic opera and theatre throughout Europe in subsequent centuries.

In print:

Odet de Turnèbe, *Satisfaction All Around (Les Contens)*
Translated with an Introduction and Notes by Donald Beecher

Annibal Caro, *The Scruffy Scoundrels (Gli Straccioni)*
Translated with an Introduction and Notes by Massimo Ciavolella
and Donald Beecher

Giovan Maria Cecchi, *The Owl (L'Assiuolo)*
Translated with an Introduction and Notes by Konrad Eisenbichler

Jean de La Taille, *The Rivals (Les Corrivaus)*
Translated with an Introduction and Notes by H.P. Clive

Alessandro Piccolomini, *Alessandro (L'Alessandro)*
Translated with an Introduction and Notes by Rita Belladonna

Gian Lorenzo Bernini, *The Impresario (Untitled)*
Translated with an Introduction and Notes by Donald Beecher and
Massimo Ciavolella

Jacques Grévin, *Taken by Surprise (Les Esbahis)*
Translated with an Introduction and Notes by Leanore Lieblein
and Russell McGillivray

In preparation:

Lope de Vega, *The Duchess of Amalfi's Steward (El mayordomo de la
duquesa de Amalfi)*
Translated with an Introduction and Notes by Cynthia Rodriguez-
Badendyck

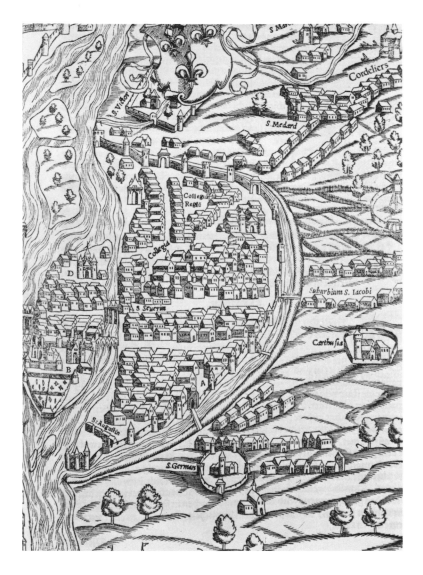

Detail from a woodcut map by Sebastian Munster, *Cosmographei* (Basle, 1550), showing the church of Saint Séverin. The Place Maubert is marked as *Collegia*. Courtesy of the Department of Rare Books and Special Collections of the McGill University Libraries.

Carleton Renaissance Plays in Translation

Jacques Grévin

TAKEN BY SURPRISE
(Les Esbahis)

Translated, with an Introduction and Notes, by
Leanore Lieblein and *Russell McGillivray*

Published for the Carleton University Centre for
Renaissance Studies and Research by

Dovehouse Editions Canada
1985

Canadian Cataloguing in Publication Data

Grévin, Jacques, 1538(?)-1570
  Taken by surprise

(Carleton Renaissance plays in translation ; 7)
Translation of: Les esbahis.
Bibliography: p. 32
ISBN 0-919473-51-2

I. Lieblein, Leanore II. McGillivray, Russell III. Title. IV. Series.

PQ1625.G6E8213 1985   842'.3   C85-090037-9

For information on distribution and for all orders write to:
    Dovehouse Editions, Canada
    32 Glen Ave.
    Ottawa, Canada
    K1S 2Z7

For further information about the series write to:
    The Editors, Carleton Renaissance Plays in Translation
    Carleton Centre for Renaissance Studies
    1812 Arts Tower
    Carleton University
    Ottawa, Canada
    K1S 5B6

Acknowledgements

We are grateful to many colleagues for their advice and support in the preparation of this play. Among them, Professors Isida Cremona and Giuseppe Di Stefano helped us to untangle difficult passages, Professors Lorris Elliott, Yehudi Lindeman and John Ripley read and commented on portions of the manuscript at various stages, Patrick Neilson made helpful comments on the final version, and Professor Pamela Stewart suggested helpful background materials. Mrs. Carol Marley, Map Curator of the Rare Books and Special Collections Department of the McGill University Libraries, helped us to find maps of sixteenth-century Paris. We are indebted to the Readers for the Canadian Federation for the Humanities who read the manuscript with scrupulous care. Their comments and suggestions have been invaluable. We also wish to thank Professor Don Beecher for his patient encouragement throughout the project. Finally, we appreciate the unfailing support at every stage and in every way of Dr. John F. Harrod.

Ms. Val Matsangos and the secretarial staff of the Department of English, McGill, remained good-humoured and helpful through numerous early drafts. The final version of the manuscript was prepared with the assistance of a grant from the Faculty of Graduate Studies and Research of McGill University.

This book has been published with the help of a grant from the Canadian Federation for the Humanities, using funds provided by the Social Sciences and Humanities Research Council of Canada.

INTRODUCTION

Life and Literary Production[1]

Jacques Grévin was born a short distance north of Paris at Clermont-en-Beauvaisis in 1538 into a family of modest means. His father died when he was young, and he was raised by his mother and an uncle, Pierre de Prong, who undertook responsibility for his education. Around 1550 or 1551 he was sent to Paris to study at the Collège de Boncourt.[2]

In Paris he entered a world of self-conscious intellectual ferment. Among his teachers were the distinguished humanist dramatist Marc-Antoine de Muret and perhaps the poet, playwright and historian George Buchanan. Among his fellow students, though a few years his senior, was Etienne Jodelle, author of the first tragedy in French on a classical model (1553).[3] Paris in the mid-1500s was the centre of impassioned debates on language and literature. The most important contemporary work of criticism is Joachim du Bellay's *Deffense et Illustration de la Langue Françoyse*, which appeared in 1549, a polemical work written in response to Sebillet's *Art poétique*, published the previous year. Du Bellay proclaimed the supremacy of classical models and urged their imitation. He was the earliest theoretician of the group of poets eventually known as the Pléiade, the most illustrious member of which was Pierre de Ronsard, the "prince of poets." Grévin was for a time associated with this group.

Around 1556 Grévin became *maître ès arts* (the equivalent of today's *bachelier ès lettres*) and was admitted to medical studies. He was awarded the Bachelor of Medicine in 1561, and although it was not then required of a practising physician, he pursued the doctorate, which was awarded in March of 1563. After that date, and until 1569, his name appears regularly among the members of the administrative council which would meet annually under the direction of the Dean to oversee the affairs of the Medical Faculty.

After his conversion to Protestantism, however, he was excluded as a result of his religious views.

The earliest survivals of Grévin's literary output, including his major writings as a poet and playwright, date from his days as a medical student. They include a number of occasional and laudatory works. The *Hymne à Monseigneur le Dauphin* honours the marriage of the future François II and Marie Stuart (1558). The *Regretz de Charles d'Austriche empereur, cinquiesme de ce nom* is a lament in the form of a prosopopeia by Charles V after his retirement to the monastery of St-Just. It was published together with a fond *Description du Beauvoisis* (1558; n.s. 1559). The *Chant de joie de la Paix* (1559) was inspired by the peace of Cateau-Cambrésis. Grévin also wrote a quasi-dramatic *Pastorale* (1559) in celebration of the marriages of Marguerite de France, sister of Henri II, to Emmanuel-Philibert, Duke of Savoy, and of Elisabeth de France, daughter of Henri II, to King Philip II of Spain. In addition, *Le Chant du Cigne* (1560; n.s. 1561), a tribute to Queen Elizabeth I, is the product of a brief stay, perhaps because of his Protestant leanings, in England. If these works show the fledgling poet in search of patronage and trying to prove himself within established literary genres and conventions, they also reveal his alertness and sensitivity to political currents and his ability to invest public occasions with genuine emotional and moral significance.[3]

The two collections of sonnets published in 1560 at the age of twenty-two reveal two sides of Grévin, for in them we hear the very different voices of the romantic idealist and the satirist. As he says in the opening sonnet of *La Gélodacrye*, "There is a time for everything, for love and for malice," and having celebrated love in *L'Olimpe*, he undertakes to sing in turn of discord and hatred in *La Gélodacrye*. *L'Olimpe* is a Petrarchan sequence in which the author speaks in conventional images of his passion, his dedication, his suffering, and, just barely, of his beloved Nicole Estienne. Nicole was the daughter of the physician and publisher Charles Estienne, himself a member of Ronsard's circle and a friend of Grévin. In fact, Estienne's translation of an Italian play may have served as a source of *Les Esbahis*. In the fashion of the time, *L'Olimpe* contains laudatory poems by no lesser lights than Ronsard, Du Bellay, and Remy Belleau. In the sonnets themselves Grévin frequently invokes these and other fellow poets and friends in rhetorical expostulation and reply. *La Gélodacrye* consists of some thirty sonnets (second parts of both *L'Olimpe* and *La Gélodacrye* are contained in the 1561 volume of *Le Théâtre de Jacques Grévin* . . .) in a Juvenalian vein. The title, coined by Grévin according to humanistic principles for expanding the French language from the Greek words for laughter and tears, suggests more balance and less bitterness than the collection actually contains. This collection of sonnets develops familiar themes: it contemplates with melancholy the human condition and denounces with bitterness (or occasionally accepts with stoic resignation) such usual objects of satire as hypocrisy and greed. It singles out for special mockery Italians, women, courtly lovers, along with lying, lecherous, self-seeking churchmen. There are also poems of prayer and of praise — of the Creation, of learning and letters, of virtue and godly living, and a few of personal longing. Thus *La Gélodacrye* is a microcosm of issues which appear in Grévin's plays and which affected his life as a Christian, a Frenchman and an artist.

The literary high point of Grévin's career comes early, with the performance on February 16, 1560 (n.s. 1561) of *César* and *Les Esbahis* at the Collège de Beauvais and the subsequent publication in June, 1561 of *Le Théâtre de Jacques Grévin de Clermont en Beauvaisis*, with a second edition in 1562. It contains Ronsard's *Discours à Jacques Grévin*, a tribute to the achievement of the volume which includes the tragedy *César* and two comedies, *La Trésorière* and *Les Esbahis*. Grévin may also have written a third comedy which does not survive, called *La Maubertine*.[4]

Grévin tells us that *La Trésorière* was commissioned by King Henri II for the marriage of his daughter, Claude de France, to Charles II, Duke of Lorraine, and that certain difficulties, which he does not specify, prevented its presentation on that occasion. It received its first performance on 5 February 1558 (n.s. 1559) at the Collège de Beauvais. The prologue to *La Trésorière* flatters the audience by telling them that they deserve better than the mélange of broad farce and religious allegory to which popular taste is accustomed. Instead the prologue promises "only antiquity." Despite his professed admiration for Plautus and Terence, Grévin's plot and its satire on women and bourgeois cupidity are closer to that of farce than he cared to admit. Constante, the Treasurer's wife, encourages two suitors: Loys, the gentleman, because of gifts, and the poorer Protonotary because she finds him attractive. Her husband returns, having been away on business, to find Loys and his servants attempting to break down the door. The rival Protonotary is inside with Constante. They are indeed caught *in flagrante delicto*, but Loys is persuaded to keep the matter silent when his gift to Constante is returned and his debt to the Treasurer at usurious interest is cancelled. The Protonotary consoles himself for the ending of his love affair by keeping the money his servant had borrowed from Constante herself, and the Treasurer, glad not to find himself in prison for usury, is reconciled with his wife. The strength of *La Trésorière* lies in the tautness of the plot and the acuteness of the satire. Its weakness comes from the blandness of the characters and the dryness of their language and characterization. Nevertheless, it is a craftsmanlike play which shows the promise *Les Esbahis* was to realize.

César is derived from a Latin play called *Julius Caesar* by Grévin's schoolmaster Marc-Antoine Muret. Although Grévin borrowed his basic structure and translated some of Muret's text, the play is his own. He altered the character and motivation of Caesar and added the figure of Marc Antony in the first act, amplified the soliloquy of Brutus and added the character of Decimus Brutus in the second act, and enlarged the dialogue between Calpurnia and her Nurse in Act III. Grévin's fourth act is entirely his own. A messenger recounts to Calpurnia the events of the murder and condemns it, and she in turn expresses her pain and longing for death. Grévin simplifies Muret's fifth act, omitting the deification of Caesar and his appearance to Calpurnia. The conspirators and Marc Antony address the soldiers who foresee that this tragic death will initiate civil discord.[5]

Perhaps Grévin's most interesting contribution is his treatment of the chorus. For a group speaking with a single voice he substitutes the individual voices of four soldiers who comment on the events of the play. This concession to verisimilitude also contributes importantly to the exploration of the theme of liberty versus tyranny.

With the publication of *César* and his comedies, Grévin was proud to bring for the first time to a reading public original plays written in French but guided, as Du Bellay had urged, by classical example. After 1562 (n.s. 1563), when he was awarded a doctorate in medicine, however, Grévin became increasingly enmeshed in religious controversy, and his subsequent publications are largely religious or scientific.

The Wars of Religion which erupted in France in 1562 and continued until 1598 brought into the open the conflict between the Huguenots and the Catholics. Protestants sought the leadership of Henri de Navarre, who was to become Henri IV. The Catholic Guises attempted, through the Queen Mother Catherine de' Medici who tried to steer a middle course, to influence the courts of Charles IX and Henri III.[6] Although Grévin died before the massive assassination of Huguenots throughout France which began in Paris on St. Bartholomew's Day, 1572, he clearly suffered for his Protestant beliefs during his lifetime. In 1563 he may have responded to Ronsard's *Discours des misères de ce temps* with the anonymous pamphlet *Le Temple de Ronsard*. His religion ultimately cost him his position in the medical faculty and his place in the work of Ronsard, who systematically erased all allusions to Grévin from later editions of his writing. It finally led him in 1567 into exile, briefly in England, then in Antwerp, and ultimately in Turin where he served as personal physician to the Duchess of Savoy and tutor to her son. During a visit to Rome in her service he wrote twenty-four sonnets which express a Protestant's antipathy for the capital of Catholicism. He died in 1570 at the age of thirty-two.

Elisabeth Lapeyre quite rightly sees Grévin among the avant garde in all of his activities.[7] As a doctor he entered the debates on the medical use of antimony (1566, 1567) and through his writings succeeded in having it banned by Parliament in 1567. He wrote against the burning of witches, taking the enlightened position that demonic possession was an illness and should be treated as such. And at a time when medical education was exclusively in Latin, he published the first anatomy text in the French language (1567). Thus Grévin in his life and work epitomizes what we have come to call the Renaissance Man.

Grévin and the Theatre of His Day

The sixteenth century was a transitional period in the development of French theatre, and the dramatists themselves were acutely aware of the innovative qualities of their work. Grévin, even more than his contemporaries, surrounded his plays with critical comments to assist, direct and appease both the readers and viewers of his plays. In dedications, prefaces and prologues, he articulated the relation of his own work to the native French drama, the dramatic traditions of ancient Greece and Rome, and the contemporary theatrical environment.

Until the sixteenth century French theatre consisted of a vigorous popular tradition comprising on the one hand religious mystery, miracle and morality plays, and on the other secular farces and *sotties*. These serious and comic theatre pieces were often performed together so that a morality play might be preceded by a *sottie* and/or a *sermon joyeux* and followed by a farce, which might also serve as a light interlude in the performance of a mystery. In the provinces, as in Paris, the plays were performed by students, clerics and artisans who formed associations of amateur actors

such as the Basochiens or Enfants sans Souci.[8] But in 1548, the
Parliament of Paris confirmed a royal privilege which had been
granted as early as 1402 by Charles VI to one of these associations,
the Confrérie de la Passion. This prevented the construction of
new theatres and entitled the Confrérie to collect fees for plays
performed publicly, whether in their own theatre or elsewhere. As
the owners of the only building in Paris used exclusively for the
performance of plays, the Confrérie had an effective stranglehold
for nearly one hundred years over the development of professional theatre in Paris. Though the Confrérie began to encounter
serious competition from numerous acting companies in the early
seventeenth century, it did not relinquish its claim to control without extensive litigation and numerous lawsuits. Paris contrasts
markedly in this respect with London where between 1576 and
1614 as many as eight new theatres plus others adapted from ex-
isting facilities housing up to at least a dozen companies were able
to compete for plays and audiences.[9] Further, although the Confrérie had control over who performed in Paris, they themselves
were hampered by another statute of 1548 which forbade the performance of religious plays. Both Catholics and Protestants were
becoming hostile to the growing extravagance of the religious
drama and uncomfortable with its mingling of the sacred and the
profane.[10] Grévin himself addresses this issue in the prologue to
La Trésorière: "For we have no intention of making religion a servant of fictions. Besides, the sacred texts were not given by God to
be turned into a play." As a result of the statute, however, the
Confrérie was left largely in possession of a repertoire of fools'
plays and farces.

Grévin does not hide his contempt for such fare. He is less
than kind to what he scathingly calls "tragédies farcées" and
"farces moralisées" which, he claims in the prologue to *Les Esbahis*,
are unworthy of a learned audience. He objects to the popular
plays on the grounds of the crudeness of their language, the bombast
of their acting, and the naiveté of their allegorical characterization.
Behind Grévin's disdain for the medieval tradition as promoted in
the popular theatres and the University lies an intellectual and aesthetic position which was developed and promoted in the colleges,
the seat of the new intellectual ferment.

The University, for Grévin, in matters theatrical at least, was a
stronghold of medievalism and conservatism. He holds it responsi-
ble, in the *Brief discours pour l'intelligence de ce théâtre* which intro-
duces his volume of plays, for committing "thousands of errors" in
theatrical practice, among them the violation of decorum, proba-

bility and the unities (*BD*, 9-10).[11] The interest in classical antiquity, and more particularly in the writing and acting of plays, took place in the colleges rather than the University itself, which was seen by the humanists as a place of intellectual stagnation.[12] Humanists objected to the sterility of the medieval form of exegesis, which emphasized formal argumentation at the expense of the interpretation of content. They also favoured the teaching of Greek and Hebrew, which the University all but ignored.[13] It was in the colleges, where leading humanists taught and wrote, that intellectual ferment and literary innovation thrived. Especially because of the interest in classical learning, drama was singled out for special attention.[14] Humanists like Grévin who wished to vitalize French literature experimented with dramatic forms, seeking inspiration from classical antiquity and observing the absorption of classical drama into vernacular plays elsewhere, especially in Italy.

This was the environment in which Grévin was a student. He was moved by the humanist programme of Du Bellay, Ronsard and others of the Pléiade to develop French language and letters by learning from the best (i.e. classical) models and educating his audiences in his methods. Thus in the *Brief discours* Grévin sees himself as an innovator precisely because he has rejected the native tradition and allowed himself to be guided by the precepts of Aristotle and Horace and to follow, among the tragedians, in the footsteps of Aeschylus, Sophocles, Euripides and Seneca. He also sees himself as part of the line of comic writing that extends from Aristotle through Menander to Plautus and Terence.[15]

Not that Grévin was alone in repudiating what he saw as the coarseness of the French dramatic heritage. As early as 1552 Etienne Jodelle, in his prologue to *L'Eugène*, claimed to be writing comedy which, in spite of its debt to traditional farce, would combine the dignity of classical comedy with the vitality of French language and experience.[16] Even more important to Grévin's work is Jodelle's *Cléopâtre captive* whose performance in 1553 Grévin may have witnessed. Grévin in fact acknowledges Jodelle in his *Brief discours* as the first to have planted the seeds of Greek and Roman tragedy in France. Nevertheless he still speaks of himself as the author of the first *original* classical tragedy in French (others before him had in fact translated some of the classical drama), perhaps because, in spite of having been preceded by Jodelle, he is the first to publish his original French plays and therefore claim the attention of a wider public.

Grévin's emphasis on publication is not a quibble. It is of a piece with his recognition that for a contribution to French letters to be genuine it must reach a wide audience and speak to its own time and place. This is the basis of his substitution of a group of veteran soldiers for the traditional chorus in *César*, a choice he defends on two grounds. The first is a question of audience: "I kept in mind that I was speaking neither to Greeks nor to Romans but to Frenchmen who take little pleasure in such singers when they perform badly" (*BD*, 7). The second raises the issue of verisimilitude: "Moreover, since tragedy is none other than a representation of truth, or that which resembles it, it seems to me that in a case where troubles (such as they describe) befall a Republic, the simple people have no great reason for singing, and therefore one should not present them as though singing in actuality" (*BD*, 7). Grévin concludes, in summary, that "different countries call for different ways of doing things" (*BD*, 7). Clearly Grévin insists on his independence from as well as his fidelity to his models.

He is similarly flexible with respect to comedy. On the one hand he insists on the classical lineage of his work. As he says in his address *Au lecteur* which precedes the comedies, "It is enough for me to offer to the French comedies of the purity that in times past Aristophanes gave the Greeks and Plautus and Terence gave the Romans" (*AL*, 50).[17] Indeed, he cites Cicero and other classical sources for the very definition of comedy as "a fictional account which nevertheless approaches truth, depicting diverse modes of life among citizens of middle rank, through which one can learn what is beneficial to life or, on the contrary, recognize what to avoid . . ." (*BD*, 7). Grévin is determined to understand the nature of classical theatrical tradition and his relation to it. He explores the distinction between Old (Aristophanic) and New (Menandrian and Roman) Comedy, and even finds the source of his hostility to native French farce in the *Mimus* or *Bastelerie* of the ancients, derided by Cicero and Quintilian because it is "composed of the vile and nasty words and lewd subjects which were also the mummers' fare" (*BD*, 8).

But even once he has claimed his comic parentage, Grévin asserts his independence, ostensibly in order the better to abide by its principles. For example, he claims that because "Comedy is a mirror of everyday life," he has allowed himself to "follow the natural idiom of our vulgar language and common mannerisms of speech rather than take the trouble to follow the example of the ancients" (*BD*, 9). It is on the matter of language that Grévin is most stridently independent of his models. In the address to his readers he argues that "the liberty of comic poets" has always permitted a freedom of language which is normally frowned upon in polite society. His humanist desire to improve the French language notwithstanding, he claims this liberty for himself, not in order to inflate or to improve upon the speech of a merchant or a servant, but for the sake of a kind of realism: "Only Comedy aims to represent the reality (*vérité*) and naturalness (*naïveté*) of the people's speech and manners" (*AL*, 49). In fact, Grévin prefers the language of the common man (*du vulgaire*) to that of the courtier (*des Courtizans*), because it does not hide its "purity" in the borrowed clothes of Latin.

In binding himself to the forms of the ancients and the language of his contemporaries Grévin allies himself with the literary and theatrical currents of his day, especially with the evolution of classical comedy as it developed in Italy. French humanists were influenced by Italian dramatists who had preceded them in the path they wished to tread, that is, to make contemporary the plays of classical antiquity. The *commedia erudita*, which reached France by the 1540s, offered a fledgling comic dramatist like Grévin a set of conventions of plot, character, language and tone. The *commedia erudita* was modeled on the basic Latin pattern of a five-act comedy of intrigue, typically set in a street or square in front of several houses and covering a period of twelve to twenty-four hours. In it ardent young men with the assistance of wily slaves or servants opposed stern or miserly fathers to gain possession of a beloved young woman (who tended to remain offstage for most of the play). It frequently employed eavesdropping, disguise, impersonation and other trickery, and the sudden removal of obstacles to the lovers' union by the unexpected resolution of questions of birth or identity. By the mid-sixteenth century the *commedia erudita* had incorporated native elements and materials from Italian life and literature. Thus the Latin parasite tended to disappear and the braggart soldier, more often than not, to become Spanish; the *senex* was made a contemporary prosperous merchant, and the slave girls and courtesans became middle-class wives and daughters who often occupied important roles in the plays. New characters from Italian life appeared, among them innkeepers, university students, and corrupt clergymen. New themes and situations — especially stories of romantic adventure: girls disguised as boys, adultery and cuckoldry, witchcraft and magic — were suggested by the increasingly popular novellas, and literary style became more self-conscious, ranging from the realistic in satiric passages to the artificial and figurative in romantic passages.[18] In addition, the *commedia dell'arte*, in which actors playing familiar characters improvised upon sketchy plots, provided a repertoire of character types and situations.

Grévin's debt to this tradition is seen in the links between *Les Esbahis* and two plays produced by the Academy of the *Intronati* in Siena, though critics disagree on whether the debt is a result of direct borrowing or of general similarities in plot and handling of the subject.[19] In fact, in his treatment of *L'Alessandro* (1544) by Piccolomini and the anonymous *Gl'Ingannati* (*The Deceived*; 1531), perhaps as translated by his friend Charles Estienne under the title of *Les Abusez* (1548), Grévin reveals the same combination of respect for and independence of his contemporary models that is present in his treatment of classical sources.

Sources

Grévin's debt to Italian comedy is great, but his departures from the sources confirm his originality and dramaturgic skill. The situations and characters he retains, while he insists on their lineage to Roman comedy in the *Brief discours*, are clearly the stock in trade of the *commedia erudita*. Common to *Gl'Ingannati*[20] and *Les Esbahis* are the old man who wishes to wed a young woman who herself is in love with a young man, the father who wishes to force his daughter into marriage against her will, and the servants who mock their masters and scheme to bring the young lovers together. Grévin made, however, a number of changes. He dropped the confusions caused by cross wooing — the girl disguised as a page who courts another woman for the beloved whom she serves — and by the mistaken identities of look-alike siblings, both of which appealed to Shakespeare when he came to write *Twelfth Night*. For them he substituted an equivalent confusion provoked by a stolen hooded cloak which enables the young man to pursue his beloved in the guise of his older rival. He also substituted for the Spanish braggart an Italian one, and for the long-lost son a long-lost wife. From *L'Alessandro*[21] too comes the comic exposure of an old man in love with a younger woman with its inevitable contrast of the sexual energy of youth with the sexual impotence of age. Through a chink in a closed door the same old man also discovers his daughter in bed with her lover whom he takes to be her fiancé because of the borrowed cloak the young man is wearing. There are also similarities, including the reappearance of specific lines and phrases, between the servants, bawds and braggarts of the two plays. But once again there are differences. Here too Grévin eliminates the woman disguised as a man in love with a man disguised as a woman, each, it turns out, the childhood lover of the other before they were separated by the hazards of war and chance.

The effect of his changes, which are related to Grévin's view of the nature of comedy, is to make the play more contemporary. Grévin consistently rejects those elements which can be called "romantic." As we shall see, when he uses disguise and recognition it is for the sake of embarrassment rather than discovery. When his lovers bemoan their fate, the extravagance of their passion is undercut by ironic reservation. Thus Grévin both simplifies his materials (reducing, for example, the number of plots contained in his sources) and satirizes them. He chooses clarity over complexity, making himself a forerunner of the neoclassicism of seventeenth-century French drama which was to win out over the Baroque penchant for elaborateness.

Grévin is of two minds about the Italian comic tradition. The products of Italian humanism were considered models of literary excellence to be admired and imitated. For example, Charles Estienne wrote in his dedicatory epistle to *Les Abusez* that Terence himself might have composed *Gl'Ingannati* had he been writing in Italian. But Estienne made it clear that the French language was quite as good as the Italian even though it had not yet given rise to great comedy. Like Estienne, Grévin clearly admired the embedding of contemporary language and setting in a classical form. The rising French nationalism, however, made inevitable a growing resistance to what began to seem like Italian cultural imperialism.[22] This would have been especially true for a Protestant like Grévin who would have associated Italianism with the hegemony of the Roman Catholic Church.

Grévin derives much from his Italian sources; however he makes his *miles gloriosus*, Spanish in the original, an Italian who is the target of endless mockery and the recipient of the Gentleman's tirade of linguistic nationalism: "Do you think French is so gross that it is less expressive than your silly effeminate tongue which, like a thick smoke, overwhelms us and ends by blowing away with the wind? Our France is fed up with your tricks and chicanery" (V.iv). In performance, of course, Pantaleone's origins would be underscored by his exaggerated accent and mannerisms.

Thus, in spite of his debt to classical and Italian drama, Grévin, who is interested in rebuilding a foundation for French letters, sees himself as an innovator and a trail blazer. He expects his two comedies to "point the way for those who will follow us." But he also recognizes the risks he is taking: "Remember it is not surprising if those who are the first to enter a desert and unknown country often lose their way" (*AL*, 50). We see then that Grévin wished to be considered original and hoped that his plays would influence his successors in the writing of French comedy. He certainly was an important part of that tradition which culminated in the comic achievement of Molière.

In the face of this it is ironic, but not surprising, that some of the features which for Grévin marked his originality in departing from his classical and Italian models are derived from the native comic tradition which he ostensibly abhorred. The title of his play is an example. It is related to *Gl'Ingannati;* the *dénouement* surprises because the characters have been deceived. But "esbahys" was also a common name for fools in the *sottie*, and *La Farce nouvelle des esbahis* is actually the title of a late fifteenth century *sottie*.[23] For the octosyllabic couplets of his verse, the proverbial richness of his language, the blatant bawdiness, and the energy of his anti-bourgeois and occasionally (especially in the speeches of Julien) anti-feminist satire he is also indebted to the native tradition of farce and *sottie*.[24]

Characters

The characters of *Les Esbahis* all belong to the comic traditions at work in the sources. For his characters Grévin draws upon the *commedia dell'arte* which was in the process of codifying the characters of Roman comedy and the *commedia erudita* into types, but he manages to imbue each of them with personal characteristics that make them believable as individuals. More than mere stylised or abstract conventions, each has his or her own personality. Furthermore, there tend to be two characters of each type. Though examples of similar duplication can be found in the sources or other plays of the genre,[25] its effect in *Les Esbahis* is to underscore the degree of individuation within the types.

Far and away the most distinctly individualized is the central figure, Josse. He is, to be sure, the Roman *senex*; he is more particularly the *vieillard amoureux* — the old man in love with a younger woman, a character who appears frequently on the French stage. The most obvious example, and the one most resembling Josse, is Molière's miser Harpagon. But while Harpagon is both odious and grotesque, Josse for all his quirkiness elicits a good measure of sympathy from the spectator. His long opening monologue presents him in all his complexity. Typical of the elderly, he rails against the times and against the fashionable youths of his day. As a *bon bourgeois* he worries about what the neighbours will say. He complains about the frivolity of women and especially of his wife (whom he believes to be dead). He bundles up against the cold even in warm weather, and later in the play defends what he imagines to be his slighted honour by resurrecting his long outmoded suit of armour. Ridiculous as he appears, he has at least a sense of honour and virtue, and his conduct throughout the play expresses his determination to find happiness — even though he is reluctant to pay good money for it. And in any case he places his happiness in an entirely unsuitable object, since Madeleine is young enough to be his daughter. Josse's essential dignity comes through despite his absurd accoutrements and occasionally cantankerous disposition. We know at once, since he and Madeleine are so ill-suited to each other, that the marriage is unlikely to come off. Yet we can hardly help feeling sorry for Josse at the end when he is forced to take back his wife, who returns to him only out of convenience. In the hands of a less sensitive dramatist, Josse would have been a cynic or a caricature. Grévin has made him not only believable with his conflicting emotions, but even an almost likeable old codger for whom we feel sympathy and a twinge of pity.

Gérard, the father of Josse's intended young bride, is obviously a counterpart to Josse. He is the other *senex*, and it is amusing indeed to hear Josse refer to Gérard as "father." But Gérard is a much less developed character and serves mainly as a foil. Lacking Josse's emotional involvement and consequent vulnerability, his ostensible concern for his daughter's welfare comes across unmistakably as a materialistic concern for his own fortune. The two old men give us the most riotously comic scene in the play, when in Act IV, Scene iv Gérard congratulates Josse on the sexual conquest which has in fact been achieved by Josse's rival. The resulting violent quarrel leads to an abortive cowardly duel (V.ii).

In addition to these two elderly bourgeois we find the common folk. The two servants, Julien and Antoine, are neatly contrasted. Julien is the schemer, plotting to outwit Josse and to assist the young lovers. Resourceful, boastful, glib, explicitly lascivious as he savours the erotic implications and consequences of the situation he manipulates, he stands in sharp contrast to the slow-witted Antoine and undercuts the veneer of bourgeois respectability of the merchants. Both the scheming *servus* and the dull-witted one are, of course, stock-in-trade figures of the comic theatre.

Two female characters are counterparts to the two servants: these are Marion the laundress and Claude the procuress. Claude is a rather shadowy figure who, like Antoine, has little influence on the action of the play. Both she and Antoine, however, are important choric voices. Antoine in Act II sees clearly the folly of his master and is the mouthpiece for conventional satiric views on marriage. Claude reinforces the note of sensuality, without which comic literature is hardly conceivable in sixteenth-century France, but her soliloquy in Act III, an ironic plea for a return to the good old-fashioned ways and means of seduction and prostitution, is an important representation of the disintegration of moral and social values, with special blame placed on the bourgeoisie. Marion is a far more developed character. She is an *entremetteuse*, and with Julien she plots and connives at every turn, boasting of her cleverness in manipulating people and events (and of course feathering her nest at the same time). She is never at a loss for the sharp rejoinder or the appropriate stratagem. The schemer or deceiver is, likewise, one of the most persistent comic types, but Marion's character is enriched by her real affection for Madeleine and a sense of the responsibility of an older woman towards a younger one whom she is initiating into the ways of the world.

The two female characters who are objects of male lust are Agnès, the wife of Josse, and Madeleine, the daughter of Gérard. It is obvious from the text that Agnès is a good deal younger than her husband. In spite of her adventurous life as the kept woman of three different men, she remains physically attractive and has lost nothing of her energy and her independence. As the railing wife — the untamed shrew — she too belongs to a readily identifiable farcical comic tradition, though her youth and sensual appeal derive from the *commedia erudita*. Madeleine is a much more colourless figure, wholly passive and "no better than she should be." She seldom appears on stage. On the surface her lamentation (II.vi) is a tissue of banalities. No doubt her thankless role indicates Grévin's scepticism regarding romantic love.

The remaining characters belong neither to the bourgeoisie nor to the lower classes. The Advocate and the Gentleman, who are cousins, are members of the nobility. It is significant that they alone of all the characters are not named and are known only by their rank. Neither is a memorable character, and they are distinguishable, one from the other, only by the woman they rely on to get the woman they pursue. It may be that Grévin shows a lack of skill in drawing them; it may also be that their lack-lustre appearance — like that of Madeleine — expresses the author's contempt for their rank and their self-seeking and self-satisfied attitude.

The last character of all stands alone, with no counterpart and in sharp contrast to all the others. He is Pantaleone, the *miles gloriosus* or braggart soldier who quails at the first hint of danger and is beaten even by the servant Julien (V.i). He is, even more, the detested foreigner. Described only as "an Italian" in the *dramatis personae*, he is accused of sodomy, the "Italian vice," and separated from the others by the distorted pronunciation of their language and the lapses into his own. A grotesque lover of Agnès and suitor of Madeleine, he is, at the end, the scapegoat blamed for the misfortunes of the others. His discomfiture represents a kind of rough and ready poetic justice. He also is the target of Grévin's obvious anti-Italian, and by extension anti-Catholic, feelings. However, even in the portrait of Pantaleone there is room for subtlety of interpretation. Grévin's learned audience might have recognized the lines of Italian as Ariosto's, and Julien's denunciation could then have reflected as much his own boorishness as Pantaleone's pomposity.

The Play

If the characters virtually all stem from a readily recognizable comic tradition, the plot too is, at least in general outline, wholly conventional. It is the common one of the young couple who, with the aid of their servants, overcome parental opposition in order to marry and so find happiness. Grévin, to be sure, treats the theme with an irony bordering on scorn. The young lovers are the most pallid of all the characters, with little individuality and no energy. It is the elders and *menu peuple* who keep things moving. The lovers consummate their union long before their marriage, which in fact is never confirmed in the play. But their attempts to come together are the pretext for the actions and counteractions of the other characters, as they are a pretext for the deployment of such comic devices as mistaken identity, speaking at cross purposes, ruse and deception.

Grévin's accomplishment lies, first, in the skilful manner in which he individualizes his characters, both in their portrayal and in the particular idiom he gives each of them to speak. The servants' speeches show an earthiness that their social betters do not have. Antoine sounds disgruntled and self-interested, while Julien is wily and cynical. They complain about their lot, as servants no doubt have always done, but when Josse complains about his lot, expressing his resentment of the abuses and privileges of gentlemen, he does so with the querulousness and garrulity of age, not with the impatient avidity of the lower classes. Grévin's considerable accomplishment, after individualizing his characters, lies in integrating them into the action. Each has his role to play. Antoine and Claude are, to be sure, episodic characters, who do more to add colour than they do to further the action, but, as we shall see, they are also thematically important. The other characters are all necessary to the plot: even the Gentleman, who at first glance appears to have no bearing on the action, is in fact the means by which Agnès can be brought on stage, foiling Josse's attempt to remarry and thus permitting the *dénouement*.

While the rhythm of the play occasionally strikes the modern reader as a little sluggish, the overall movement is steady and regular, with all the acts neatly balanced both as to length and as to importance. The action respects the dramatic unities. All characters and events revolve around the central subject: the efforts of the young couple, aided by the servants, to circumvent an unwanted marriage.

The monologues which serve chiefly to introduce the characters are an important part of Grévin's dramatic method. They are of the moralizing kind common to late Renaissance and Baroque theatre, and though their function in Grévin's play is chiefly expository, their effect is complex. This process is not unlike the one to be found a century later in the full flood of French classical drama — lengthy presentation of character rather than of action or subject is a common feature of Molière's expositions also. That Grévin has made a deliberate choice to begin his play with a long and, perhaps to modern ears, static speech is clear from the fact that he altered his source to do so. Nor is such an opening likely to be a sign of the immaturity of Grévin's dramaturgy, since he had already shown in *La Trésorière* his ability to introduce a play with an effective dialogue of exposition.

The key to the stage-worthiness of Grévin's monologues lies in their tone which imposes upon the audience a specific relationship to the characters and events of the play and gives to the long speeches an important dramatic function. The theatre-goer who listens to Josse's opening monologue is not, as in the case of a soliloquy, in the privileged position of overhearing the expression of his innermost thoughts. Rather, the spectator is directly addressed and invited to experience the speaker's vulnerability and sense of genuine injury. Josse as an old man in love with a young girl and a merchant in love with his money would have been a recognizable composite type from Italian learned comedy to the college audience before whom *Les Esbahis* was originally performed. Nevertheless, Grévin takes the daring step of having a character who is unsympathetic by definition of his type invite a potentially hostile audience to share his bourgeois view. Josse speaks of his wife and his money as possessions equally subject to exploitation by gentlemen courtiers, and as their victim, he communicates a sense of genuine injury. Not that Grévin ultimately wishes us to identify with Josse. Perhaps the Prologue's warning not to let Josse suspect anything separates us from him and invites us to exclude him from our sympathy. Certainly the subsequent entrance of Marion deflates his pretensions and confirms his ridiculousness, but not before the audience has had a chance to take his quandary seriously.

The dramatic monologue of Marion works against that of Josse with which it is juxtaposed by revealing the gap between his expectations of Madeleine's love and their chances of fulfilment. Marion's description of Josse's physical appearance permits the audience to step back for a second look at the man whom they had previously been encouraged to view through his own eyes. This technique of raising sympathies and expectations, then undercutting them by way of juxtaposition, is central to the organization of Grévin's play. We see it in the placing back to back of Act II, Scene vi and Act III, Scene i. The innocent Madeleine's lament on the fate of her love in a hostile and materialistic world is followed by the lament of the experienced bawd Claude on the falling off of her business. It is used more subtly in Act IV, Scene vi, where the Advocate and the Gentleman refuse to listen to each other as each tries to impress the other with the praises of his newly conquered mistress. In the praises that each sings there is no discernible difference between the romantic ingenue Madeleine and the whorish Agnès. Similarly, the self-importance of the Italian braggart-lover Pantaleone is undercut by Julien's derision. Grévin's characters assume that the audience shares their values. In their monologues we hear, as Grévin promised us in his *Au lecteur*, their voices and their views. But the lovers are forced to abandon their pretensions: Josse is reduced to the comic fool, and Madeleine and the Advocate give up their rhetoric of love for the real thing.

Basically, such contrasts expose the inadequacy of the romantic view. Lute-playing, Ariosto-quoting Pantaleone is the grossest distortion of the courtly lover. Mocked for his foreignness, isolated by his language, and exposed for his cowardice, his wooing is all posture and gesture. But at a time when the Petrarchanism of earlier poets was being rejected, the diction of Madeleine and the Advocate would also have suggested the inauthenticity of their passion.

The play adopts the romantic comic convention of siding with the young lovers, but only insofar as their pragmatism wins out over their idealism. The Advocate's wooing of Madeleine is no more substantial than the braggart's until Marion's intervention brings about the consummation of his love. The play similarly exploits the romantic convention of reuniting long lost relatives, but with an ironic twist. Josse, the would-be lover, does battle for honour, but for his own, not the beloved's. As the would-be husband, he gets a wife but not the one he wooed. He is restored to his long-lost wife, but only after she has been mistress to three different men and makes clear that she intends to preserve her freedom. Instead of married bliss he can look forward to a life of married misery. Even the untidiness of the ending contributes to our sense that Grévin is unable to adopt without reservation the conventions of romantic comedy. The marriage of the Advocate and Madeleine is perhaps assumed but it is never confirmed, and Gérard still believes Julien's assertion that it was Pantaleone who disguised himself in Josse's cloak.[26]

Thus practicality, common sense, and allegiance to community win out over pretension and self-aggrandizement, and it is the servants and socially marginal characters who possess the former qualities in the greatest abundance. Marion and Antoine reminisce (in II.v) about the good old days when Agnès presided over a household of good cheer, and regret the cupidity and materialism of the present. Dame Claude longs for a better time when people were more sexually active and less eager to take over her profession, and Julien places himself at the service of members of the audience and professes his willingness to help them as lovers. According to the theatrical convention on which Grévin is drawing, the cleverness of the servants and go-betweens is taken for granted, but the low-born characters, who are active, put their energy at the disposal of the essentially passive upper-class figures.

Both groups have in common their regret that times have changed. Their nostalgia is made more poignant by the care with which Grévin paints the present. For example, each of the characters is socially placed with precision, even in the list of *dramatis personae*. They are merchant, servant, or gentleman, laundress, lawyer or bawd, and in such things as their clothes (the lawyer's "bonnet rond") and their speech, they bear the marks of their class. However in their actions and aspirations the servants are allied with the gentlemen and the women against their merchant masters. Gérard and Josse, though they bear the mark of the Roman *senex*, are more than the heavy father and pantaloon lover. They are newly moneyed men whose human feelings (as husband and father) have been distorted by their materialism and whose isolation and impotence are comically reflected in the scene in which they speak at cross purposes. Furthermore, the degeneration of human values in the domestic sphere is mirrored in the military and political upheavals which are capable of destroying fortunes and breaking up families.

A glance at Grévin's English counterparts helps to clarify the nature of his dramatic imagination. Grévin has more in common with such Jacobean playwrights of urban life as Dekker and Middleton than he does with Shakespeare who was drawn to the same source with very different results. In *Twelfth Night* Shakespeare transforms the disguises and mistaken identities into the instruments and processes of self-knowledge and personal growth. In contrast, Grévin's Advocate learns nothing when he disguises himself in the stolen cloak of Josse. He gets something, however: possession of Madeleine, whom Gérard had agreed to transfer to Josse.

In all of this the complicity of the audience is assumed. From the prologue, where the audience is asked not to let Josse suspect anything, to the epilogue, where the audience is urged to satisfy the sexual longings which the play may have aroused, it is in the privileged position of having more information than at least some of the characters and therefore of being able to enjoy the author's dramatic irony.

This is reinforced by the setting of the play which is an extension of the world of the audience. The sense of place and of time in *Les Esbahis* is precise and elaborate. While the prologue of *Gl'Ingannati* (as of Estienne's translation) makes clear that "this city is Modena, the time this year, and the people who take part in the story are most of them Modenesi," Grévin's comedy is set not only in Paris but more precisely in the vicinity of the Place Maubert, and hits so close to home that he courts the risk, as his Prologue says, of having his audience believe (and resent) that they are his subject: "He hasn't even dared to write the name of the street where he witnessed these events, because he was afraid of provoking the women. However, I found out from him — but it's a great secret — that this comedy tells about a love affair which took place at the Carrefour Saint-Séverin." Thus the public square of Italian

comedy, an imaginary space permitting the natural arrival and de-
parture of the players as well as eavesdropping and fortuitous or
necessary encounters, is here replaced by a real city space, in the
Saint-Séverin district of Paris only a few steps from the Sorbonne
(and from the Collège de Beauvais where the play was first performed. See the frontispiece map for a sixteenth-century view of
this quarter). The characters (with the exception of the outlandish
Pantaleone) and the setting are all recognizably and quintessen-
tially French, despite the conventional stylisation of the plot, and
the play is squarely placed in contemporary Paris. The Prologue
thus mediates between the illusion of the play and the "reality" of
the audience's situation. Not only does he imply that the love affairs the play recounts actually happened, but also, as Josse enters,
that it is happening right now: "But I must ask you to be quiet if
you wish to be let in on it, for I see Master Josse coming up behind
me; don't anyone let him suspect anything. For you know he's got
engaged since he's convinced Madame Agnès is dead." Hence the
playwright draws the audience into the web of his play by making
claims on their complicity. In painting his satiric portraits he draws
on their anti-bourgeois and xenophobic sentiments.[27] At the same
time he succeeds in creating rich individuals in a tightly wrought
comic play which anticipates the classical theatre of the seventeenth century.

Above all, Grévin's comedy is eminently playable. The characters are sufficiently likeable and sufficiently ridiculous to be amusing, and they are believable. The action never drags, and even the
monologues have their dramatic function. There are no redun-
dancies and no vacuous or pointless scenes. Although French theatre was still tentatively seeking its way, burdened as it was with humanistic erudition and lacking professional players and adequate
theatre buildings, Grévin's comedy strikes the modern reader as
sprightly, full of wit and good humour, moving naturally and
swiftly through the twists and turns of the plot. It is a thoroughly
theatrical piece of theatre.

The Play in Performance

The play was first performed — presumably before students and
teachers, although Wiley suggests the possibility of a wider audience[28] — at the Collège de Beauvais in Paris on February 16, 1560
(n.s. 1561). It was presented together with the tragedy *César* and

the "jeux satiriques" *Les Veaux*, in an attempt to imitate the comprehensive dramatic presentations of the ancients.

There is no certainty of what this first performance was like, but some suggestions emerge from historical documents and the text. A description of Etienne Jodelle's *La Rencontre* and *Cléopâtre* at the Collège de Boncourt, possibly witnessed by Grévin in 1552, with people hanging out of the windows to watch it, implies an outdoor or courtyard performance: "This comedy [*La Rencontre: The Encounter*], and *Cléopâtre*, were performed before King Henri [II] in the Hôtel de Reims, and were well applauded by all those present. They were performed again at the Collège de Boncourt, where the windows were filled with a multitude of distinguished persons and the courtyard was so full of students that the doors of the college could scarcely be shut."[29] Grévin's allusion to an "eschaffault" in *La Trésorière* seems to suggest a scaffold or stage constructed for the occasion. Although Grévin would have been familiar with Serlio's 1545 designs for a comic stage setting which included a church and the houses of a merchant, a courtesan, and four citizens, and although the play could have made use of such a setting with separate houses (entrances) for Josse, Gérard, Marion, Claude, and so on, *Les Esbahis* makes much less complex specific demands, requiring only Gérard's house which the disguised Advocate enters and beneath whose upper window the Italian serenades. Although there are allusions to other houses, they are not required for the action on the stage, the most important place of action being, in the Roman tradition, a generalized street. Thus although Grévin insists on a specific locale in his prologue, he relies on his text rather than on his stage to create it, and his play could have been performed if necessary on a relatively bare stage containing a single "mansion" or compartment, or in front of a wall or façade containing at least one door and, perhaps, a window or gallery.[30]

Grévin in fact uses the convention of a public street or square as a central acting space to great effect. Whatever its physical dimensions may have been, he permits his stage to accommodate several characters or groups who may be unaware of each other's presence at one time. Thus the Prologue is able to enjoin secrecy from the audience as Josse enters. Similarly, Marion's opening monologue, which follows Josse's, is strengthened by the fact that Josse probably remains on the stage. Though they are initially unaware of each other, her ludicrous description of his appearance both before and after his falling in love with Madeleine is underscored by his physical presence and could well be enhanced by gestures of preening on his part. Similarly, in Act II, Scene iii, Julien enlists the hostility of the audience against Pantaleone by deriding him as he continues to serenade his beloved Madeleine on the stage.

The fact that the "public" space of the stage is not bounded also permits the characters not only to address the audience directly, but also to make competing claims on its sympathy. Thus in Act I, Scene iii both Antoine and Marion use asides to assert confidently that each will worm secrets out of the other, while in Act II, Scene iv Julien overhears Marion's resentment that his master, the Advocate, has supposedly betrayed Madeleine, and braces himself, in asides, for her assault. More importantly, Grévin uses the street effectively as the place of chance encounter between Madeleine's father and the Advocate disguised in Josse's cloak as he triumphantly steals away from his beloved's bedroom.

The flexibility of a neutral public space containing one or more specific locations contributes to the fluidity of *Les Esbahis*. Thus when the stage at one moment in Act V is dominated by the grouping of Josse, Gérard, Pantaleone and their servants and the next by the Gentleman, Agnès and the Advocate, we have a sense of movement in time and space, even though the two groups may occupy in succession the same area of the stage. At the same time Grévin skilfully uses the presence of Julien in both groups to create continuity.

Control of the tempo of his play contributes as well to the effectiveness of Grévin's dramaturgy. The long opening speeches are followed by a succession of dialogues of scheming on behalf of the young lovers, that is, delaying tactics to keep the old men at bay. The implementation of the scheme of the Advocate's disguise in Act III accelerates the confrontations. Even characters who would prefer to avoid each other cannot help meeting. The Advocate flees Gérard. Marion tries to keep Gérard and Josse from understanding each other. The Gentleman and the Advocate are eager to recount their sexual adventures but not to listen to each other. The stage in fact becomes progressively noisier and busier as it moves through the recriminations and mock duel between Gérard and Josse to the apprehension of Pantaleone and the forced reconciliation of Josse and Agnès. The play concludes with no fewer than six characters on the stage, at least half of them "taken by surprise."

Elaborate stage business contributes to the vitality and stage-worthiness of *Les Esbahis*. Even with a minimal set (and there is no way of knowing how spare or decorated the set may have been), it is likely to have been a visually impressive play. The social status of the bawd, the servant, the laundress, the merchant and the Gentleman would probably have been clear from their costumes, as would the foreignness and foppishness of Pantaleone. The Advocate's "bonnet rond" is clearly specified. So are the preposterous furs worn by Josse and his old-fashioned suit of clothes carried by Antoine to be altered, stolen by Marion, and worn as a disguise by the Advocate. Josse prepares himself to duel in a rusty suit of armour. There is much bravado, comic cowardice and bandying about of staves in both the duel and in Julien's baiting of Pantaleone. And of course there is Pantaleone himself with his everpresent lute, his musical set pieces and the familiarly exaggerated gestures and manner of the braggart.

All of these "bits" are specified by Grévin's text. They are only a starting point for actors already exposed to the conventions of performance of farce, *commedia erudita* and *commedia dell'arte* as Grévin's contemporaries most likely were. Indeed, in its skilful manipulation of the time-honoured conventions of comedy Grévin's play would probably prove its theatrical viability even before a modern audience.

History of the Text

Les Esbahis was originally published in 1561 in LE THÉÂTRE DE JACQUES GRÉVIN (Paris: Vincent Sertenas and Guillaume Barbé). A second edition, with numerous minor corrections, appeared in 1562. In addition there exists in Antwerp a copy of the second edition, undoubtedly brought there by Grévin himself in 1567, which contains alterations to some 200 lines in the author's own hand, in general to modernize, regularize or to improve upon language and versification. The play was reprinted in the nineteenth century in Volume IV of *L'Ancien Théâtre François* (Paris: P. Jannet, 1855) and was included in Lucien Pinvert's *Théâtre complet et poésies choisies* (Paris: Librairie Garnier Frères, 1922).[31] Most recently, Elisabeth Lapeyre has produced for the "Société Des Textes Français Modernes" an excellent critical edition with introduction and notes of *La Trésorière* and *Les Esbahis* (Paris: Librairie Honoré Champion, 1980).

The Translation

For the present translation we have consulted the editions of Pinvert and Lapeyre as well as copies of the 1561 edition in the Bibliothèque Nationale, and have used Lapeyre's, based on the 1561 version, as the authoritative text. Where they have made a difference to the meaning, we have taken into account Grévin's corrections in the Antwerp copy and indicated the variants in the notes. We have also relied extensively on the introduction, notes, and glossary of Lapeyre, to whom our great debt will be apparent.

Grévin's text was stage-worthy in his own time and remains so today. The play is written in rhyming octosyllabic couplets, the most common verse form used in sixteenth-century French comedy. The rhyme scheme and strong rhythmic pattern impart energy and vitality to the spoken French text, and Grévin avoids monotony (though not always confusion) through his long sentences and skilful use of enjambment. The same verse form, a flexible instrument in sixteenth-century French, would sound over-emphatic to the modern ear. Therefore, we have attempted in our translation to preserve the qualities of Grévin's language, which is energetic, colloquial, rhythmically varied, and heavily laced with proverbs, in contemporary, idiomatic English prose. We have endeavoured to remain faithful to the original and to convey, as Grévin does, the individuality of his characters through their speech idioms. We have tried to avoid, however, slang or levels of diction which would too soon date, and have striven for a flexible stage language which an actor could give meaning to. Thus we have on occasion found it necessary to break up Grévin's long sentences into smaller syntactic units and to change their order to make them seem more natural in English. Sometimes we have translated literally and less than colloquially to retain the metaphoric texture of the original; at other times we have departed from the original in our search for a modern equivalent. All such departures and their literal alternatives are indicated in the notes. While we have deleted the quotation marks which indicate proverbial expressions in the original as incompatible with modern usage, we have attempted to keep their proverbial flavour in our translation.

We have kept the French names of the characters, though we have modernized their spelling which, in the original, is on occasion inconsistent. For example, Madeleine's name appears both as Madalene and, in its more affectionate form, as Madelon. Though the usage roughly corresponds to the tone of respect or intimacy with which she is being referred to or addressed, Grévin readily abandons the appropriate form for the sake of the rhyme. For the convenience of the reader we have added minimal stage directions in square brackets to help clarify entrances, exits, and asides. Stage directions in parentheses are Lapeyre's. On the whole, however, we have striven to let Grévin's text speak to the modern reader as it did to his contemporaries.

NOTES TO THE INTRODUCTION

1 For further biographical information see Lucien Pinvert, *Jacques Grévin, étude biographique et littéraire* (Paris, 1899); Lucien Pinvert "Notice sur Grévin," *Théâtre complet et poésies choisies de Jacques Grévin* (Paris, 1922), v-xlix; William Beck, "The Theatre of Jacques Grévin," Diss. Rutgers 1964; Elisabeth Lapeyre, ed., *Jacques Grévin: La Trésorière, Les Esbahis*, Société des Textes Français Modernes (Paris, 1980), ix-xiv. The present discussion is indebted to all of these studies.

2 Or possibly the Collège de Beauvais. The biographers are uncertain. Grévin's associations with Muret, Buchanan and Jodelle suggest Boncourt, but his plays were performed at Beauvais which tended to attract students from Grévin's native region.

3 The first original tragedy in French was *Abraham Sacrifiant*, written in 1550 by Théodore de Bèze and performed in Lausanne. It employs such classical elements as a chorus, but in his use of a biblical subject and such characters as Satan and an angel, Bèze was chiefly adapting the tradition of the medieval mystery play to his own Calvinist purposes.

4 Brian Jeffery, *French Renaissance Comedy 1552-1630* (Oxford, 1969), 185-86, proposes that *La Maubertine*, which Pinvert thought to be another name for *La Trésorière*, is a separate play.

5 Jeffrey Foster, ed., *"César" de Jacques Grévin: Édition critique avec introduction et des notes* (Paris, 1974), 14-21. See also Jacques Grévin, *"César": Édition critique avec introduction et notes*, ed. Ellen S. Ginsberg, Textes Littéraires Français (Genève, 1971), 20-45, for a full discussion of Grévin's sources.

6 For more information on the historical background see James Westfall Thompson, *The Wars of Religion in France 1559-1576* (1909; Rpt. New York, 1957).

7 Lapeyre, xiii.

8 L.-V. Gofflot, *Le Théâtre au collège du moyen âge à nos jours* (Paris, 1907), 21; W.L. Wiley, *The Early Public Theatre in France* (Cambridge, 1960), 32.

9 *Annals of English Drama 975-1700*, ed. Alfred Harbage, Rev. S. Schoenbaum (London, 1964), 297-306.

10 Wiley, 146. For more background to sixteenth-century French drama see Grace Frank, *The Medieval French Drama* (London, 1954), Richard Axton,

11 The *Brief discours* is reprinted in Pinvert, ed., *Théâtre complet*, 5-10. This edition is cited in the text with the page number as *BD*. The *Brief discours* can also be found in Bernard Weinberg, *Critical Prefaces of the French Renaissance* (Evanston, Ill., 1950), 184-88.

12 The colleges were originally established, usually through bequests, as hostels or residences for needy students. The most celebrated, though not the oldest, was the Collège de Sorbonne, founded about 1257 by Robert de Sorbon to house students in theology. As the University of Paris had no buildings of its own, professors soon began to lecture in the colleges, which accordingly became, in effect, seats of learning. By the 16th century they had grown numerous and some had become centres for humanist studies. Chief among these colleges were the Collège de Boncourt (founded in 1353) and the Collège de Coqueret (founded in 1463), where certain of the future Pléiade poets studied under Jean Dorat (or Daurat).

13 I.D. McFarlane, *A Literary History of France: Renaissance France 1470-1589* (London & Tonbridge / New York, 1974), 25. See also Raoul Morçay and Armand Müller, *La Renaissance* (Paris, 1960), 123-28, and Anne Denieul-Cormier, *La France de la Renaissance 1488-1559* (n.p., 1962), 367.

14 Wiley, 35, also cites the promotion of drama in the Jesuit colleges. Founded in the spirit of the Counter-Reformation, the Society of Jesus "wanted to vivify religion, avoid the abstraction of the Sorbonne in their instruction, and to make study a pleasure." See also Madeleine Lazard, *Le Théâtre en France au XVIe siècle* (Paris, 1980), 89-92.

15 Bernard Weinberg, "The Sources of Grévin's Ideas on Comedy and Tragedy," *Modern Philology*, 45 (1947), 53, demonstrates that, in spite of his claims, "essentially, there is no theory of the dramatic art in Grévin's preface; there is merely a re-echoing of the standard tradition." While this may be true of Grévin's "theory," his translation of critical theory into practice breaks new ground.

16 McFarlane, 444.

17 Reprinted in Pinvert, ed., *Théâtre complet*, and cited with the page number from this edition in the text as *AL*. Also reprinted in Weinberg, *Critical Prefaces*, 188-89.

18 For this summary we are indebted to Philip Wadsworth, *Molière and the Italian Theatrical Tradition* (n.p., 1977), 5-6.

19 Lapeyre, xxxi-xxxiv, summarizes the controversy.

20 Though Grévin was certainly aware of the French version by Charles Estienne (there is some resemblance between the critical argument in the prefatory epistles) he was assuredly familiar with the Italian original as well, since he retains the figure of the Spanish braggart (though he makes him Italian) whom Estienne deletes.

21 We are indebted to Rita Belladonna for permission to consult the manuscript of her edition of *Alessandro*, No. 5 in this series. *Gl'Ingannati* can be

found in English translation in *Five Italian Renaissance Comedies*, ed. Bruce Penman (Baltimore, 1978) and in *The Genius of the Italian Theater*, ed. Eric Bentley (New York, 1964).

22 An example of the movement away from Italian sources can be seen in the changing attitude among poets of the Pléiade toward Petrarch. Henri Chamard, *Histoire de la Pléiade*, 4 vols. (Paris, 1939-40), in I, 222-79; II, 120-61, 209-13; III, 228-29, 360-62, passim, documents this shift.

23 Heather Arden, *Fools' Plays: A Study of Satire in the Sottie* (Cambridge, 1980), 41.

24 Jeffery, 15, 160; Lapeyre, xlii. Arden, Chapter Four, passim, discusses the anti-feminism of the *sottie*. In contrast, Belladonna, in her introduction to *Alessandro*, 9, 12 suggests that the large number of women present at Italian Academy performances contributed to the development of women's roles in the *commedia erudita*. Grévin's own attitude seems ambivalent. His Prologue attacks the women of the Place Maubert (though perhaps tongue-in-cheek), and he gives traditional scathing anti-feminist remarks to Antoine and Julien. These, however, are servants and may express the popular disparaging attitude towards women rather than Grévin's own view. Moreover, he creates in *Les Esbahis* a wide range of interesting and attractive, if conventional, female characters.

25 Lapeyre, xxxvii-xxxviii.

26 Jeffery, 123.

27 Grévin directs his barbs chiefly against Italians whose presence at the court of Catherine de' Medici, widow of Henri II and Queen Regent, was a constant irritant.

28 Wiley, 32-36.

29 Translated from Etienne Pasquier's description of the event as quoted in Jeffery, 69.

30 See Jeffery, 54-74, for an excellent summary of evidence relating to the staging of sixteenth-century plays.

31 Lapeyre, xlv-xlvi, lxxiii-lxxiv.

SELECT BIBLIOGRAPHY

Beck, William. "The Theatre of Jacques Grévin." Diss. Rutgers, 1964.

Jeffery, Brian. *French Renaissance Comedy 1552-1630*. Oxford, 1969.

Herrick, Marvin T. *Comic Theory in the Sixteenth Century*. Urbana, 1964.

Lazard, Madeleine. *La Comédie humaniste au XVIe siècle et ses personnages*. Paris, 1978.

Lazard, Madeleine. *Le Théâtre en France au XVIe siècle*. Paris, 1980.

Lebègue, Raymond. *Le Théâtre comique en France de Pathelin à Mélite*. Paris, 1972.

McFarlane, I.D. *A Literary History of France: Renaissance France 1470-1589*. London & Tonbridge / New York, 1974.

Pinvert, Lucien. *Jacques Grévin, étude biographique et littéraire*. Paris, 1899.

Stone, Donald Jr. *France in the Sixteenth Century: A Medieval Society Transformed*. Englewood Cliffs, New Jersey, 1969.

Weinberg, Bernard. "The Sources of Grévin's Ideas on Comedy and Tragedy." *Modern Philology*, 45 (1947), 46-53.

Wiley, W.L. *The Early Public Theatre in France*. Cambridge, 1960.

TAKEN BY SURPRISE
(Les Esbahis)

a comedy

DRAMATIS PERSONAE

JOSSE, a merchant

MARION, a laundress

ANTOINE, servant [to Josse]

ADVOCATE [in love with Madeleine]

GENTLEMAN [his cousin, in love with Agnès]

JULIEN, servant [to the Advocate]

PANTALEONE, an Italian

MADELEINE, daughter to Gérard

CLAUDE, a bawd

GERARD, a merchant

AGNES, wife to Josse

Note: Words in square brackets have been added by the translators. Stage directions in round brackets appear in Lapeyre's edition.

PROLOGUE

I haven't come here to tell you, in detail, the story of our Comedy.
You're probably in the mood to hear us and watch us play our
parts, and I don't want things to be spoiled for you before you've
seen the play.

I've been sent here by the Poet himself to tell you what, more
than anything, bothers him. First, it's that people put up with these
nitwits who'll try any trick[1] to ingratiate themselves with the University.[2] They're a rag-tag troupe who make a mockery of verse.
Nothing but impudent rhyming hacks. They chase after the muse
who's all the rage, but just make fools of themselves. These upstart
actors[3] are still wet behind the ears, so they try to whip up the
passions in their farcical tragedies and moralizing farces. They use
trumpets and drums and crude words that offend the ear[4] to instil
pity or woe[5] into the heart of the most attentive spectator instead
of doing it by means of good poetry.

One other matter brings me here, and that's to remind you
that the women in this part of town, out of anger and resentment,
have recently lodged a complaint against the Poet. These ladies are
so touchy they make a mountain out of a molehill. When you least
expect it they take offense at the most innocent remark. They turn
the Poet's attempts to entertain you into a personal affront. And if
a new comedy happens to make mention of the Place Maubert,
they always imagine it's referring to them.[6]

What I'm trying to say is that the Poet has been cautious in
writing his lines for the Comedy you're about to see. Still, he
wanted to tell you the story of these oh so happy love affairs,
though he hasn't dared mention the name of the street where he
witnessed the events, in order to avoid provoking anyone. Just the
same I found out from him — mind you, it's a great secret — that
this comedy tells of a love affair that took place at the Carrefour
Saint-Séverin.[7] But I must ask you to be quiet if you want to be let
in on it, for I see Master Josse coming up behind me: don't let him
suspect anything. You know, he's got himself engaged, since he's

long been convinced that Madame Agnès is dead. But before he makes his exit, you'll learn all about his troubles.

ACT 1

SCENE I

JOSSE *(Alone)*

JOSSE: Never would I have thought I'd be so poorly repaid in the end. To lose my wife and my money and on top of that the market for my best merchandise. But such are the times we live in. Over and over, ever and always, this is how these courtly types settle their bills, and they never leave without their loot. They think that all worthy men steal the way they do. And, poor as we arc, we have to put up with these so-called gentlemen. From morning to night-time they lean on our counters, chat up our wives, and even while they take such liberties they rattle on about nothing.[8] We might as well sleep the morning away, because these gallants do our work for us better than if we'd done it ourselves. And for such an act of charity, I leave you to imagine how they pay us back. God in heaven. Meanwhile justice turns a deaf ear, and if it happens that one of these wife-molesters does get caught, you can imagine how the whole stupid neighbourhood will laugh. You know this little game is no fun for those who are the first to suffer from such insults. The most reasonable man alive couldn't endure torture like this without losing his patience. Only someone who has had the experience can know what it's like — and he can't prevent it. Because the more you try to protect yourself, the more shamelessly these scoundrels look for a way to slip out of your clutches. There's nothing so tempting as forbidden fruit. But why beat your head against a wall? If a woman's taken the step once, she's always ready for another try; it's a point of conscience never to refuse the pleasure of that dearest possession of hers to any poor lovesick fellow who comes along.

That's how this impudent woman first went astray, and now from that moment I've been more miserable than ever before. Once she began her galavanting and let the cat into the cream pot,[9] she neglected the household duties and I was never the wiser for her betrayal. She brought into my house her scoundrelly lover[10] who knew only too well how to make a profit from my assets. When he saw the moment was right, he used my misfortunes as a pretext, and he pretended to help me out, showing himself entirely too eager to save my wife, my money and the best of my belongings as if they were his very own.

But in times of trouble one must keep heart. I've learned a thing or two from my unhappiness. In fact, I consider myself even more fortunate than I would ever have dreamed. After a spell of bad fortune, you often find unexpected reward with the help of good friends.

My neighbour, Gérard, has been assuring me that the promised wedding with Madeleine, my fiancée, will take place one of these days. But it seems to me she's dragging her heels a bit.[11] You'd think you were flaying her alive when you speak of the marriage. If there isn't more to hope for from this love of mine than there is from the dowry my father-in-law promised, I would never have proposed. But then she's just a silly little child. I'm sure that she doesn't know what it is to feel the pangs of love, and that only bashfulness makes her shy away. She's still a young and tender creature and, by heaven, all things considered, the torment I've known is really nothing when I think of the comfort I'll take in her arms. For that's how love grows stronger.[12]

SCENE II

MARION, JOSSE

MARION: [*Without seeing Josse*] Since the day Master Josse got engaged to Madeleine, he's become more spiteful and proud and more conceited than if he'd dropped down from heaven. He used to be dirtier and grimier than an old shoe — scruffier and more worn out too. His jowls used to hang down half a foot on either side; he looked like the devil himself. To see him so shabby and grubby, you'd have taken him for a corpse. Who do you think could have loved him? But since they told him his poor wife is dead, he's changed completely — turned

himself inside out and forgotten his grief. Now he obeys his
Madeleine better than a horse obeys the spur. But he'd do better to look for someone else. Engaged to her or not, I can tell
you she's not the one for him. And that's why I've got something in store for him today. He'd better not think he's going
to make off with the prize that a better man deserves. She
worships at another shrine. I'd really love to see another man
hunt in Master Josse's place, but first I'll get from him the
hood he promised, then wait for my chance for something
even better from the young lover. After all, you've got to look
after yourself.[13]

JOSSE: [*Aside*] Isn't this my laundress? Yes, by St. John, it's her all
right.

MARION: [*Aside*] Here comes Josse, paler than a two-week old ca-
daver — a real champion in love who imagines he's still up to
it! He could fuel a fire, but he couldn't put it out. He still
thinks he can get what he's aiming at, but has he ever got a
surprise in store. He might as well give up. Just look at this old
rotten stump near a fire that's too hot for the best of men to
handle.

JOSSE: Well, well, here's Marion, my sweet, light of my life, my
heart's delight. Tell me, then, how's my little Madeleine?

MARION: Couldn't be better.

JOSSE: I love her to distraction.

MARION: And she loves you.

JOSSE: Ah, Marion, I love her so; I can never be happy unless I
have news of her.

MARION: She certainly is one of the beauties in the neighbourhood.

JOSSE: Yes she is, yes she is.

MARION: But one thing bothers her. Your clothes are all wrong.
Here you are, dressed in fur when it isn't even cold.

JOSSE: It's to guard against a fluxion of the lungs that I had recently. I keep the kitchen warmer than usual, but just the
same, what with a cold and coughing all night, I was in such a
state that I nearly gave up the ghost.

MARION: And with that you imagine a wife can be happy with you?

JOSSE: I'm sure this cough of mine will leave me soon, Marion.

MARION: [*Aside*] If you ask me, it's a cough that leads to the grave.
—It's the best thing there is about you.[14]

JOSSE: Old dogs hunt best. Besides when all is said and done, I'm
not as old as they think. Believe me, I'm in the very prime of
my life, I assure you, and still full of fight. You yourself can
swear to it. You remember what we did behind the door, when

I made you work for your wages. I was ready to go for a second lap, but you told me I was too hot for another try and once was enough.[15]

MARION: Saint Peter! What I said was just to make you feel good, because you couldn't have come out of it with your honour the second time.

JOSSE: Even so, there isn't a man alive who can do his duty better than I can.

MARION: To hear you tell it, you're quite the adventurer.

JOSSE: I am. And gallant enough to enjoy myself when I wait on my Madeleine in bed.

MARION: With one look at you [Aside] — even though your eyes are runny —anyone can see how handsome you are.

JOSSE: I can still get it up. Maybe I don't have much colour in my cheeks, but my rod is as hard as any you could ask for.[16]

MARION: You're one of those who talk a lot but don't do much. You're too nice to bite.[17]

JOSSE: I'll manage things so well, you can be sure we'll have a fine time. I'm in good form and there's no need to spur a horse that's already chafing at the bit.

MARION: But what about the hat that you promised me so long ago?

JOSSE: Marion, you can count on me and Master Gérard as your friends. Believe me, you'll get your reward, since by your help I'm going to enjoy the pleasure I've been waiting so long for. We'll all be satisfied in the end, don't you worry.

MARION: But answer me plainly: shall I have the hat or not? Have you forgotten it?

JOSSE: Here are two crowns for you, Marion. Buy anything you want.

MARION: What's this? Your hand is trembling. Are you forsworn in love?[18]

JOSSE: I do believe that when words fail you, Marion, the Seine will run dry. You always have a sharp comeback.

MARION: Why shouldn't I? Am I the only one today who's looking for a little fun? I swear, so long as I know how to have a good time, I'll make out. When I die, everyone will be dead to me.

JOSSE: It's the same for me. I know that Madeleine just wants to enjoy herself and all I want is to have a laugh now and then.

MARION: She'll make you feel good. She has no patience with melancholy and will add ten years to your life. And let me warn you of something else: she's expecting to have a family too.

JOSSE: That's another reason I've been trying to find a way to win her, not for her dowry, but for my pleasure. Believe you me, that's the truth.

MARION: You only get what you pay for.[19]

JOSSE: Well Marion, let's go and see her, because I want to ask how she's feeling. I can't be happy unless I see her with my own eyes.

MARION: This isn't the right time, take my word for it.

JOSSE: Then I have to go on waiting without talking to her?

MARION: Trust me to bring you news of her. I'm doing everything possible to put an end to your misery. I have an even greater desire than you do to see you two together. So, cheer up. You know you have to encourage these young brides. She's just sent me to call for her friends to come and gossip and dine with her and, to tell you the truth, it seems to me better to leave them to themselves, either to sing or to dance or to talk about love all day long.

JOSSE: If you say so. And while I wait for the wedding, remember me to Madeleine, and tell her she can expect to really find someone to talk to then.

MARION: You'd better learn to dance in the meantime. You don't want to miss out on the fun when that day comes.

JOSSE: Of course not. And I'm sure that Madeleine will be ready to show off what she can do too.

MARION: And she'll do it all to please you; but you'll certainly have to do your part. Farewell, Master Josse.

JOSSE: One more word.

MARION: Well, what is it?

JOSSE: I can't keep from rejoicing. Greet her for me.

MARION: Indeed I will. [*Exit Josse*] I'll see to it that the designs of this toothless old fox come to nothing. However wide he opens his mouth, he won't get a morsel. The wares are already sold to a merchant who will take the lot. He doesn't stand a chance, since I intend to stop him.

Just think how I'll enjoy seeing a lusty young man get the goods that someone else tried hard to get. This ancient withered spectre, this cur, this screech-owl, this Hydra who could serve as a lantern if he had a fire in him,[20] is a perfect scarecrow of death. He insists on playing the gallant even though he leaks at the nose and the eyes. Good God, her father, Master Gérard, should blush for shame to take so little account of her. May I never move an inch if I don't tell him so. To look at him, you'd think he was an old cow who'd never kicked up her heels as a heifer.[21] A curse on whoever thought to concoct such a match. People are sure to gossip.

SCENE III

ANTOINE, MARION

ANTOINE: [*Without seeing Marion*] So help me God, I can't keep still about it. Since this fool, my master, has fallen in love, there's not a moment's peace in the house. There's such coming and going, it's enough to drive you crazy.

He parades by himself and mutters about the household he expects to set up soon; he doesn't even forget to plan the privies. One minute he washes his face, the next he curls his hair. He pretends to play the lover to his little kitten, whispering sweet nothings to it as though it were a young girl. Then he says: here is the chamber where Madeleine will learn how babies are made. Suddenly, he becomes frenzied, grinds his teeth, rolls his eyes, and shouting so loud that we all tremble, he summons us together: "William, come and comb my hair. You, to the cook with you, and you, off to the caterer. And you, go see if my cape, my long cloak and my old doublet have been altered to fit me." As for me, being the most trustworthy, my job is to bring news of him to Madeleine. But the unmistakable news I get from her, from the way she acts, is that she doesn't care a pin for him. But this I keep to myself, since I know better than to open my mouth. If I did otherwise, you can imagine the kind of welcome I'd get.

In front of her door is a preening Italian with a lute that's out of tune. You can't miss him, since he makes a habit of coming every night. There's another young man in a round cap[22] who looks as though he'd as soon kiss his neighbour as a total stranger — it's all the same to him. I hear that for a long time he's been after her to get some reward for his pains. He's begging the laundress for help, and will do almost anything to ease his turmoil. And I honestly believe — unless the proverb lies — that Madeleine won't fail him, because it's in the nature of things: "a girl is always ready to follow in her mother's footsteps." And that's as it should be.

MARION: [*Aside*] Who's that talking so loud? It's Antoine, Master Josse's servant, just the one I wanted. Watch me worm his secrets out of him. I'll see if I can't get him on our side.

ANTOINE: [*Aside*] Here's Marion. I'd better watch what I say and see
if I can't learn something from her. I want to know what's up.

MARION: [*Aside*] He'd better watch out; never try to outsmart someone who's as smart as you. I'm convinced that he's coming
here to see if we'll say something to give ourselves away, but
I'll manage things so cleverly that I'll find out what he's trying
to do.

ANTOINE: [*Aside*] I think Marion's waiting for me.

MARION: Well, well Antoine, where are you going?

ANTOINE: Don't you know that we're always running back and
forth?

MARION: For your love-sick master?

ANTOINE: For him all right. He's become so strange that unless he
changes soon, he'll drive the lot of us crazy. But I'm hoping to
take revenge on his madness, if I can. I swear he's talked my
head off, and his tongue's not half long enough for the rest of
his life.

MARION: It's love that makes him act this way.

ANTOINE: Until his desires are satisfied, it's all that we're likely to
see. He raises Cain if any of the five of us servants wants to
rest a bit. Believe me, the gentry were never so difficult as
these petty merchants, these silly, vain fools who claim to be in
love.

MARION: Antoine, if I were to ask your help in this affair of mine,
could we work something out?

ANTOINE: Nothing would please me more. Out of love for you I'd
do anything. If there's a trick to be turned, I'm the readiest
man in the world to give you a helping hand.

MARION: All right, that's all I wanted to hear. I'm ready if you are.
A friend in need is a friend indeed.

ANTOINE: Don't worry. You can count on me, if only for her[23] sake.
Enough said. Trust me.

MARION: And you me. Where are you going in such a rush?

ANTOINE: I have to fetch a suit at the tailor's. When I get back we'll
talk further.

MARION: [*Aside*] This is no time to stand around doing nothing.
There's so much I have to do. I'd better tell the young man
about this, he's all worked up about it. [*Exit*]

ANTOINE: By heaven, I think any man a big fool who takes it into
his head and makes up his mind to get married. He's planning
something that won't do any good. If he marries a rich
woman, she'll lord it over him. If he marries a poor one, then
what misery! He'll become her servant, and where before he

was living quite happily, instead of one mouth to feed he now has two. And if he picks an ugly one, he'll have no pleasure in her. If she's fair, she is sure to make a cuckold of him. In some nook or cranny, off on a side, a neighbour will get in his licks. So, whoever decides to settle down can never escape this absurd law of a woman's nature. The man who gets married is like a mule tied up all day without hay, his mouth gaping at the manger.

ACT II

SCENE I

ADVOCATE *(Alone)*

ADVOCATE: Such long perseverance — and is my reward then to be forgotten? Is my devotion to be repaid with injustice? Now I see how little faith and how much treachery lie in the feigned promises of a mistress. The soft allure and sweet words, the fair charms and winning ways which made me her prisoner, concealed her false love. They hid her faithlessness so well that, though they mocked me, I noticed nothing. So well did they deceive me that they triumph over my shame and hold me captive to the god of love.

Ah, Madeleine, who would have believed that once our love began, strengthened by our vows as it was, it would suffer such change? Ah faithless promise! Shortlived vow! A promise that becomes a lie when the promised goal is not in sight. Now come and sing praises to the faith of women; nay, respect and honour them — and receive for such labour grief beyond compare. Their insincere passion reveals nothing of the design they hide behind their so-called weakness. Just turn your back, and they'll speak the same words to the first man[24] who comes along. All the while they hold you in thrall with the cunning of their sweet blandishments.

My Madeleine, whom I loved more than my heart, than my eyes, for whose love I died a hundred times a day, I vowed my heart to you alone like a true servant. You who accepted my homage and swore to be true forever — already you have forgotten me and have broken faith and are content to take as your fiancé an old man of fifty.

SCENE II

JULIEN, GENTLEMAN, ADVOCATE

JULIEN: No, no, sir, he's wasting his time. There's no use in his being angry, it's all settled. He might as well give up once and for all, for I've seen Master Gérard who was talking about it to the cook. You can be absolutely sure of it: tomorrow at the latest Josse will be her husband.

GENTLEMAN: Heaven knows, I'm as disturbed about it as he is himself; for though the misfortune is his, I feel it as my own. Isn't that him I see coming? We must find a way to release him from his chains.

ADVOCATE: [*Aside*] I'm so upset that I can't concentrate on anything else.

GENTLEMAN: Well, my friend, how is your heart doing now? Are you going to let love make a slave of you? Speak up. Can't you govern your desires any better than this? Little by little you've got to put out this flame that's consuming you.

ADVOCATE: Ah cousin! It's easy enough for you who are well to give advice to an afflicted man. Had you felt the pangs of love as I have done — but I'll say no more.

GENTLEMAN: Enough of that, I know what you mean. But you should remember that the best way to avenge yourself for the trick this heartless woman has played is to take as little account of her as she does of you. From now on, like the rest of us, choose them one day at a time.

ADVOCATE: Ah cousin, she is too noble to be so easily forgotten. I took pleasure in the torment, seeing my freedom conquered by such a fair one.[25]

GENTLEMAN: I admit she's fair, and had it not been for the love and friendship we have for each other, I might have fallen in love with her myself. But now that she has become engaged, banish her from your thoughts. You must seek your fortune elsewhere.

ADVOCATE: Never. I swear I'll be her servant forever. Never will I set my heart on fire for another.

GENTLEMAN: There's lots of good fish in the sea.[26] Remember that there are other beautiful women you can fall in love with. Someone else can win your heart and make you her willing servant. Don't forget that Paris is full of women who would gladly be yours. How they'd love to set your heart on fire and make you a slave to their beauty. Your pursuit of Madeleine

gave you nothing but grief, one minute agitated, moping the
next, first eager, then reluctant, dying fifty times a day for
love of her. Even when she smiled at you, her favour was
short-lived. Her uncertainty should have warned you what
would come of it.

ADVOCATE: Cousin, the more I strive to resist her, the more my torment grows; I think I shall surely die of grief.

JULIEN: [*Aside*] He'll never leave her. Love has shackled him hand
and foot.[27] If she were to set out on the high seas with sail and
oars, these flames of desire would drive her back to port in
spite of all her efforts.[28]

GENTLEMAN: Well, since this woman has drained your blood and
spirit, and tames you, we must find a way for you to get her.

ADVOCATE: But tell me, Julien, what does the laundress have to
say?

JULIEN: Still beseeching you in the name of your Madeleine. She
says that it was the spiteful father who forced his daughter
with threats, and that her heartfelt grief clearly shows how she
regrets her inconstancy. She feels quite miserable.

GENTLEMAN: It's time to shut the stable door when the horse has
run away!

JULIEN: She's unhappy enough as it is. What we have to do is look
for a way to snarl things up and put a stop to this business.

ADVOCATE: All right, if you can do it.

JULIEN: Leave it to me, I'll see to it. A serious illness calls for strong
medicine. And if Julien doesn't always come up with a way out
I'd like to hear about it. I'll show you what I can do in a case
like this and how ready I am to spend my life looking out for
the person I serve. There isn't anything I wouldn't do in this
affair, and besides, its merit spurs me on to do even more.
This will prove I just want to be useful to such a fine master
and help him out of his tight spot.

ADVOCATE: And I give you my word, Julien, that[29] if I can enjoy
Madeleine, your reward will be as great as the trust I placed in
you when you entered my service.

JULIEN: Generosity encourages faithfulness in obedient servants.
But let's not talk about enjoyment yet. Promises can come
later. For now the laundress is the only one who can help me.

ADVOCATE: Even if I have to abduct her, it's worth risking my honour for.

JULIEN: It's not a question of abduction if the girl is willing. And if
there's to be an abduction, I'm sure I can pull one off as
quickly as anyone.

GENTLEMAN: It's all in your hands now.

JULIEN: I'll look after everything. At the least, if I do things right, he'll have the first go at her in repayment for his love.

GENTLEMAN: Off you go, Julien, and on your way back stop off at Claude's and see whether she has anything for me. I'm surprised she hasn't come back. [*Exit*]

JULIEN: [*Alone*] The blind man thinks of his walking stick all the time, and the seaman, after he runs aground, tells you how dangerous the winds were; the cowherd, when he comes from the fields, talks about his oxen, and the soldier, after a dangerous skirmish, tells you about his wounds. The shepherd remembers how many sheep he counted. That's how things go. Starting isn't the same as finishing. Marion's a sharp one, and I've got her work cut out for her. But what I like best of all is that she's as shrewd as any woman in Paris and knows how to find you a naked girl for your bed. I've heard this from husbands, who have often tried out the goods she sells. And since she's a laundress, she gets the dirty linen clean. Anyone who needs her services will find her in some corner or other, though he better not try her patience just for the sake of testing her. But enough of that. I must find her in any case. Julien, if you have your wits, now is the time to put this mess to rights.

SCENE III

PANTALEONE, JULIEN

PANTALEONE: [*Without seeing Julien*] Ah, what a mighty thing love is. It torments me night and day. My suffering knows no end. God in heaven! If only Madeleine knew of my grief. I am sure that her heart would pity my distress, in despetto of her ancient father, who will not permit my entreaty to reach Madeleine's ears, despetto of her wicked father and the young advocate as well, who causes me all my grief and misery. But I solemnly vow from this moment forth to seek some other means.

JULIEN: [*Aside*] Well well, here's our Italian fellow. Messer Poltroon himself.

PANTALEONE: Ah lord, my sorrow is extreme. I see only cruelty in this all-conquering god.

JULIEN: [Aside] It's not for you, you wretch, that the oven is getting hot.

PANTALEONE: Oh what pain and torment is the lot of poor Pantaleone.

JULIEN: [Aside] Poor lovesick fellow!

PANTALEONE: Since my misery comes from the fair eyes of my heartless mistress, only Madeleine will relieve my pain.

JULIEN: [Aside] You lie, you scoundrel.

PANTALEONE: Still, what pleases me most of all is her grace and her beauty. Her cruelty means nothing to me, since I serve so noble a lady.

JULIEN: [Aside] Just look at this brave Messerre! To see him you'd think that the ground isn't worthy enough to bear him. Soon you'll hear him boast; soon he'll brag about his exploits and tell you about those he defeated when he conquered a chicken coop. He'll tell you what a brave warrior he is when it comes to breaking down an open door or plunging his hands into a meat pie.

See him picking his teeth? He's emptied his helmet for dinner and kicked up his heels for dessert.[30] Yet here he is, blithe and merry, at Master Gérard's door, playing the lover. He'll be in a real mess if Master Gérard ever learns of it and can find him. Sticks would have to cost a lot for him to get off without a beating. He'll be sent off with his tail between his legs.[31] By heaven, if they find him here he'll rue the day he began carrying on like this. Master Gérard isn't one to put up with such an insult.

PANTALEONE: Per riaver l'ingegno mio m'è aviso
che non bisogna che per l'aria io poggi
nel cerchio de la luna o in paradiso;
che 'l mio non credo che tanto alto alloggi.
Ne' bei vostri occhi e nel sereno viso,
nel sen d'avorio e alabastrini poggi
se ne va errando; et io con queste labbia
lo corrò, se vi par ch'io lo riabbia.[32]

JULIEN: [Aside] Wretches, slaves, poltroons. Sidekicks of St. Anthony. May you catch the disease of St. Lazarus[33] and the falling sickness too.

SCENE IV

MARION, JULIEN

MARION: [*Without seeing Julien*] What a shame it is! I can't imagine what kind of love's around nowadays; our Advocate, who always seemed the model lover, has become another person. I have the feeling he's done an about-face.

JULIEN: [*Aside*] Marion!

MARION: In the meantime poor Madeleine suffers more than ever, and her love gets stronger by the day as the wedding approaches. I'll really tell him off — this fine gentleman who is nowhere to be found when we need him; he's a coward in love and not the man I thought he was. His servant, who promised me yesterday that he would meet me at mass to speak to both of us, didn't keep his word.

JULIEN: [*Aside*] Oh-oh, Julien, she has it in for you.

MARION: The poor girl can't bear it any more. She weeps all day, and she's in despair to see how little she matters to him. He should be ashamed of himself to go back on his word. But isn't that Julien coming? He's looking this way.

JULIEN: I must say, Marion, a man can never catch you off your guard.

MARION: Don't you realize what's happened? We have to try something else. Now's not the time for shearing sheep. Do you know what? I need you to help me out of this mess. We must find a way to trick this fellow who's coming towards us.[34]

JULIEN: He looks as though he's daydreaming and is half out of his wits.[35]

MARION: It's one of Josse's servants. They haven't had a minute's rest since this mismatch was announced.

JULIEN: But Marion, what do you expect to get out of him?

MARION: This is how we'll do it. Here's my plan. By hook or by crook, I'll borrow the cloak he's carrying, and believe me, if he gives it to us, your master will have a cozy time of it if he goes along with me. First, in this borrowed disguise, I'll bring him into Madeleine's bedchamber, where the tender young thing won't be so unfeeling as to resist a kiss or two. She won't be too shy to submit easily to such a pleasant form of pain on the corner of her bed. And come what may, when Gérard finds out, he'll have only himself to blame for having been taken in by such a ruse.

JULIEN: And so he'll have his tumble, let the worst come to the worst.

MARION: We must find a way to get him[36] to come and eat something at my house. Meanwhile, go home and tell your master to come to my place right away.

SCENE V

ANTOINE, MARION

ANTOINE: [*Aside*] There she is. There's my laundress who's always the first sign of a new love affair. She's never still, day in and day out all the month long.

MARION: [*Aside*] Oho! As clever as you think you are, you won't escape from me. I'd better be careful, gullible though he is.

ANTOINE: Well, Marion, what do you want to talk to me about?

MARION: Antoine, my son, my good lord, my sweety, I invite you to come and have a bite with me. For I swear that I long to dine with you more than you can imagine.

ANTOINE: That's all right with me. If you fancy it, so do I. What I want most in the world is to have a good time and take things as they come.

MARION: Antoine, when I remember how much I have to put up with, I could cry. Where are the great times when Dame Agnès, your mistress (may God forgive her sins), made sure we had the best wine, and took pleasure in laughing and making us happy when we were off work? Ah me, those were the good old days. Nowadays, people talk about nothing but money. Nothing in your house is as good as it used to be; things have changed a lot. I'm convinced you put up with more torment, trouble and pain on the best day of the week, than you used to have in a full year.

ANTOINE: Marion, our luck has turned, but I hope in future to laugh harder than ever.

MARION: Come, Antoine, let's go in.

SCENE VI

MADELEINE *(Alone)*

MADELEINE: Ah, will the flower of my youth be lost forever and the joy that I hoped for come to nothing through this unyielding fear of mine? Now I feel the power of love. But alas, my help-lessness, and threats and promises, have put me to such an-guish that as soon as I resolve to do something, honour at once opposes it. If it didn't mean more to me than life itself, and if I believed my heart, my love and my honour would be one. Only one man will enjoy the fruits of his long persever-ance, and it won't be a toothless dotard who doesn't deserve to enjoy them and never will, come what may. Dear Heaven! How a father deceives himself when he thinks he can restrain his child's wishes. Because he has eyes only for money, he imposes on both men and the gods. We have the power to consent to pleasure of our own free will, or we ought to have it, but he deprives us of it.

Most of the time they bargain as though they were selling a horse to the highest bidder. And who gives the most and wants the least is given first refusal of the match which, in any case, will not be granted right away, because they are waiting for someone who, if at all possible, won't ask for so much. Be-sides we always see the kind of love that is sure to follow from such an arrangement:[37] marriage with someone you never saw before you became engaged. But it's useless to complain of my misfortune. I blame my faint heart and my heedless tongue which alone are the cause of my misery. Ah, Gracious Virgin. How can I bear the grief I have to endure? The waiting and hoping that filled my life are gone. Greed, constraint, injus-tice, harshness and cruelty have snatched away pleasure and freedom and the one I loved most of all. How can I show my-self to the heavens? Can I, who am guilty of such inconstancy, come into their presence? Will the earth bear me? Will the air refresh me with its sweet breath without tormenting me? May unkind nature and a guilty conscience punish me forever for my inconstancy. Let love do with me what it will, for before I so injure my beloved, death alone shall avenge my weakness as an example to posterity.

ACT III

SCENE I

CLAUDE(*Alone*)

CLAUDE: I don't understand these times. You know courtiers are colder and paler than the mouth of a corpse. Everyone remains buttoned up and no one calls on my services any more. And believe me, if one of them happens to take his pleasure, I get only as much as he's willing to spend. Things aren't what they used to be.

I used to find that if someone wanted a rendez-vous there was always a little dinner money in it. Meanwhile, the lady was ready and waiting, and what a reception she gave him as long as the money kept coming in. But today, the devil take them. They're only snot-nosed kids, but they'll pester you a thousand times on the slightest pretext.[38] And as soon as you grumble a bit, they scowl and threaten you. And you'd better not go back on any of your promises, for they know how to get even. Then when it's time for them to leave, they don't pay you a red cent. You get threats and arrogance, an "I defy" or "I deny". Just try to earn a living when they run out on you instead of paying,[39] and are likely to greet you at night with a volley of insults. That's how things are with me now. And since they all know me, they never cease shouting and banging on my door as if they were going to break it down. This has been going on for the last two weeks, ever since they heard the rumour that Dame Agnès is at my place. But I swear a solemn oath (and I wouldn't perjure myself) that I will manage my affairs so well that no protonotary or courtier, however fine he is, will dare to look at the roof of my house without paying for the pleasure.[40] And if the malcontents want to do it themselves, I wash my hands of it.[41]

I don't know how long it's been since this trouble started, but the world isn't what it used to be. At one time any old soldier, however poor and ignorant, would come and sharpen his tool when he returned from battle. But nowadays poor love is billeted in the richest houses. There's not a burgher's wife in town who can't scheme as well as any bawd to find her own love. She pretends to meet her cousin, and what's more, gives money to her suitor, and the best wine to drink, or gives him clothes to make sure the arrangement holds. Or she tries out the goods under cover of marriage in order to save her reputation. The devil with such assignations. They manage everything themselves, and this is how our profession suffers, where we used to have plenty of clients. And what bothers me most is that the competition keeps increasing. Today there's no part of town that doesn't have a hundred doing my work. You can see even the wealthiest trafficking in their kinsmen in the hope of an abbey or some other high office for a reward, and you can forget about finding justice.

SCENE II

GENTLEMAN, CLAUDE

GENTLEMAN: There's no two ways about it. Anyone who wants a little fun nowadays with Dame Holy[42] must first announce it to the whole convent if he doesn't want to find them all on their backs. When one of them is ready, Dame Claude says the time's not right, so that oftener than not you come back empty-handed. Even when there is plenty to be had, the woman isn't in the mood when you are, and when you don't feel like it, that's all she thinks about. But I don't feel like coming here for nothing; that would be paying fifty times more than it's worth for the pleasure. Why, this bawd is readier to take care of some fool of a stranger than she is of her friends. A client's always put off till tomorrow, while the stranger who just came along always finds a woman at his disposal, for she doesn't want to lose his money. She's done it to me. I'm telling you, if you don't know all the tricks of this trade you're likely to pay for it if you make a blunder. If you don't grease the palm of everybody in sight,[43] you're always put off until another day. You have to know how to please everyone. And God knows how they swear up and down to hide their tricks.

But here comes sweetness itself. She seems to be sure of herself from that determined look of hers. I'd better not waste any time.

CLAUDE: God keep you, sir.

GENTLEMAN: And you, Claude. How have you been lately? Things seem to be going better than they were a while ago.

CLAUDE: They're not as bad as they were. You know, sir, all the money I manage to put aside — and it isn't easy — is gobbled up in a week. But however bad things are, I'll always find good things like lard pastry to eat.

GENTLEMAN: And so you should. You're clever enough to get as much again.

CLAUDE: Believe me, if you're content, you're happier than the King. What do I have to worry about? There's only myself, and I swear to heaven that as long as I have my wits about me, I'm not afraid I'll die of hunger. Every day[44] brings its bread.

GENTLEMAN: That's how it should be. Why worry yourself to death about the things of this world? Besides, one is never the richer for fifty pounds of trouble.

CLAUDE: I'll never be stingy as long as I have a penny in my pocket.[45] It's foolish to fret about worldly goods and torture yourself with what is to become of you in this life. The wisest are those who have the fewest cares.

GENTLEMAN: Come, Claude, let's get to the point. You haven't said a word about that. Have you arranged something? The rendez-vous is set for today. What's the next step?

CLAUDE: Believe me, I was just on my way to find you; and if it hadn't been for my love for you, I could already have received ten crowns, with the expectation of more, for the girl.[46]

GENTLEMAN: But who is she?

CLAUDE: Ah sir, she's the most beautiful woman you ever laid eyes on. And what's more, her graciousness and honesty are a perfect match for her beauty.

GENTLEMAN: [Aside] Some churchman's leftovers, I'll bet.

CLAUDE: Yet I can assure you that she's not the kind who'll run after a man just for his money. And she's not one of your calculating hussies who think only of worming what they can out of anybody who comes along.

GENTLEMAN: Where did you find her? How did you get to know her so well? Tell me how it happened.

CLAUDE: I'll tell you. Remember three years ago the French were driven out of Saint Quentin,[47] and the Parisians were dismayed to learn that people were fleeing and that Picardy was in ruins. So everyone did what he could in order to save his belongings and to avoid the impending danger. It happened that a man from Gascony, who had escaped from the field, knew a certain Master Josse, an important merchant in this city. The Gascon knew that Josse had a fat purse, and he pretended to accompany his wife, whose beauty probably excited him. But to tell the truth, the money excited him even more. Then, on my word, he carried her off to Lyons[48] and left her high and dry, with only his empty promises.[49] The fellow kept the money, abandoned her there, and hurried off home. So she was left on her own, but since she was a beauty, she was soon taken up by a young Italian.[50] He found her fresh and lovely, and took his pleasure with her for three full years. Two months ago, as he had business with a Frenchman of this city, he brought her with him, and she has been staying in the house of one of his close friends in Saint-Germain-des-Prés. Yesterday she came to see me, since she used to come quite often. She told me that the Italian hadn't been to see her for at least two weeks and that she had run away. In any event, she is at my place, safe from the clutches of those jealous Italians.

GENTLEMAN: But tell me Claude, how much will it be to have a look at her?

CLAUDE: I'll have to think about it. To look will cost you nothing. And let me tell you, I'm sure that you'll want her more than once.

GENTLEMAN: She'll find that a Frenchman is as lively and as ready as any Italian.

CLAUDE: Well then, let's go. And I'm certain that you'll find this filly as lively and as ready as any Frenchwoman, however boastful you may be.

GENTLEMAN: Good. When I'm amorous, I need to be satisfied at once, without torturing myself endlessly with suffering and sighing and a thousand romantic entanglements.

SCENE III

JULIEN, ADVOCATE

JULIEN: You know, Sir, when you're on the attack, you must show yourself a man of courage. Fortune smiles on lovers.

ADVOCATE: I feel my courage and strength growing greater and greater; I feel my love is daring enough to meet the wildest

enemy. I feel like Jove. When he was aroused he would sometimes forsake his thunder and lightning for similar pleasures
to content his amorous heart. Once, in a passionate mood, he
disguised himself to sire his glorious son Hercules.[51] Love[52] is
never dismayed. It can always invent a thousand ways to
satisfy its longing. And once a lady learns of the amorous
flame which torments and consumes the heart of her faithful
servant, she will contrive a thousand ways to lighten [53] the
heavy chains of his martyrdom.

JULIEN: Do you feel confident, since you're the aggressor, that
you'll bring off a victory today? At least convince us that you
are, even if nothing should come of it.

ADVOCATE: No, no I'm certain that if I can get inside, there will be
good sport either by love or by force.

JULIEN: The first step is always the hardest. Believe me, if I were in
your situation I'd be sure to do the best I could. But I believe
what you say. I'm sure the first few stabs will be the riskiest.

ADVOCATE: Julien, did you see the Italian come past here?

JULIEN: Who? That swaggerer? By God, he's wasting his time. I spit
on him, the coward. Marion finds him amusing. She entertains
herself with him.

ADVOCATE: Well, he'll be sorry if I ever get my hands on him.

JULIEN: If nothing else I'll get his cape and hat and pay him for
them with a few blows.

ADVOCATE: Come on, Julien, enough of this Italian.

SCENE IV

MARION [carrying Josse's cloak], ADVOCATE, JULIEN

MARION: I've got my gallant[54] so drunk that he's snoring away. This
will give us plenty of time to do what we have to do.

ADVOCATE: So, Marion, how's our affair going?

MARION: For goodness sake, get a move on. You should have been
back by now.

ADVOCATE: What do you mean? If I were recognized, they'd act as
if I were raping her.

MARION: There's nothing to worry about, you can rely on me. Besides, Master Gérard has just gone downtown, and even if a
thousand people were to see you, none of them would recognize you.

ADVOCATE: You're quite right, Marion. But does Madeleine agree?

MARION: How can you ask? It's what she's waiting for. Come on, follow me. [*Gives him the cloak which he puts on*]

JULIEN: Meanwhile I'll wait here, sir, and leave her to you. And tell her to let me know how she made out.

ADVOCATE: Still harebrained, aren't you. Won't you ever behave?

JULIEN: Come on, sir, be brave.

ADVOCATE: Marion, do you realize how much better suited to turn a trick a man is when he's dressed in clothes like these? A monk's habit can also be very useful for disguising a woman and bringing her more secretly into a monastery.

MARION: Mum's the word. We're nearing the house, sir. Conceal your face with the corner of your cape.

JULIEN: His impatience is getting the better of him.

MARION: Hurry up, then. Enter as confidently as if it were your own house, and just let one step follow the other.

JULIEN: [*Alone*] So you see, all it takes is imagination to arrange a rendez-vous and satisfy one's longings. A woman knows more sleights and shifts of love affairs and lovers than a thousand men. There's nothing of these matters which she doesn't know about. On the other hand, to tell the truth, there is no creature in the world worse than she is for spoiling a promising affair, if she puts her mind to it. If she doesn't bring off all the tricks she sets her hand to, she gets sick and positively miserable. But if you want to avoid that, you have to try and get around women the right way, and flatter them, and promise them the moon. If you can't afford to pay them, they'll go more than half way with you if they take a liking to you, and there's no danger in getting them right into bed. That brings them around even faster. Everybody says that in Paris you have to win over the husband before the wife. Indeed you do, and if you're even more clever, you'll win over the bawds as well, if you want to have the prettiest ones, because that's how things are these days.

SCENE V

GERARD, JULIEN, MARION

GERARD: I hope to goodness this marriage works out well and that it leads to as much joy and happiness as it began with. If anything went wrong with it I would be very sorry to see Madeleine suffer while she is in the flower and springtime of her youth.

JULIEN: [*Aside*] My God, my master is betrayed. The game's up. Here's Gérard.

MARION: [*Returning*] May the good Lord give them time enough to satisfy the anguish of their passion. He's inside and was far enough along when I left him, so it seems; he could hardly wait to get his clothes off. I doubt there remains any quarrel between them that hasn't been settled by now.[55]

JULIEN: Well, how does it look? How did she receive him?

MARION: Couldn't have been better.

JULIEN: But now what? Here's Gérard.

MARION: Mercy on me! Shh. Don't say a word; I'll find a way to save everything. You, Julien, go and wait for your master at my house; he'll follow you there.

JULIEN: I will. But if he catches them in the act, it's all up with us. [*Exit Julien*]

MARION: Don't worry about it. I'll see to everything.

GERARD: Here's Marion. She seems pretty worried about something.

MARION: I beg your pardon, sir, but what are you doing here when you should be seeing to the preparations for the banquet? You know servants never do anything without their master, who can get more for a couple of crowns than they can for half a dozen.

GERARD: I have seen to it; but has Madeleine got over her sulk?

MARION: For goodness' sake, it was just that she was afraid of leaving you.

GERARD: What I did was only for her own good. I also want her to obey me as a child should her father.[56] What pleases me should please her, and she should want what I want.

MARION: You shouldn't be so harsh, for gentleness can do much to move a girl's heart, in fact much more than if you try to abuse her feelings.

GERARD: I know. If I hadn't wanted her to come round of her own accord, I would have taken care of this long ago.[57] But to marry in haste is to repent at leisure. Therefore I wanted to wait for the right moment so as not to regret anything. Now I want to tell her about it. Let's go do it together.

MARION: Let them talk a little. Master Josse is in there.

GERARD: I wonder why I didn't meet him on the way?

MARION: I think that Madeleine is scolding him for being so negligent.

GERARD: Why? Because he doesn't come to see her often enough?

MARION: Exactly, take my word for it. They were kissing, I saw them myself. What more do you want? She's the one who led him on.

GERARD: Then I hope to heaven it's for the good of both of them. Come, let's talk to them.

MARION: Wait here at the entrance. I'll go up to the bedroom and call them.

GERARD: Good idea.

MARION: [*Aside*] Mercy on me, what shall I do now? I'll have to sharpen my wits.

ACT IV

SCENE I

ADVOCATE [*Still wearing Josse's cloak*]

ADVOCATE: *(Alone)*[58] Long live love and the lover who has satisfied his longings and ended all his torment! Long live the lover who wishes to die such a sweet death! Compared with this pleasure, my suffering, my passion, my sorrows, and all the torment I endured while courting her count as nothing. In spite of what I imagined, I see that my perseverence is now rewarded. I used to sigh and tremble in fear. But ever since this noble hope came to spur me on, fearless love has rewarded me for my suffering. My desire for glory made me certain of victory in the most perilous combat. And now I see that my hope did not deceive me, because a merciful lady, when she saw a poor and miserable wretch, was not too hard of heart to take pity on her lover. That is why, so long as my spirit moves me and while my heart beats strong, I will expose my honour, my body, my goods, my very life to an enemy's sword, for a lady true of heart.[59]

SCENE II

GERARD, ADVOCATE

GERARD: Hold on, Master Josse, my friend,[60] a word with you. Come over here. What are you afraid of?
ADVOCATE: [*Aside*] What shall I do? How can I keep so great a joy to myself? Where is my cousin?
GERARD: Hello friend. Tell me, neighbour. Haven't you done enough talking?

ADVOCATE: [*Aside*] Dressed as I am, I hardly dare take two steps for fear of meeting someone I know. I'd better go to Marion's. I want to avoid any more trouble.

GERARD: Hey there, come back.

ADVOCATE: [*Aside*] Oho, you won't catch me. Who'd have thought you were so near? Goodbye, Gérard, goodbye. [*Exit*]

GERARD: I do believe my neighbour Josse is getting more vigorous by the day,[61] ever since this promise of marriage. He used to be pensive, listless, and slow to take the initiative, and today he can't get enough of it. Well, believe me, I'm glad of it.

I was peeking through a gap in the bedroom door, and I saw him in bed with my daughter Madeleine. I'm convinced he was enjoying it as heartily as a young man would in his place. He's sure to do even better in the future! Even though the wedding is just a short time off he can't wait to put a bun in the oven.[62]

SCENE III

ANTOINE, JOSSE

ANTOINE: [*Without seeing Josse*] I'm afraid I'll be beaten for taking so long; my master's an absolute devil whenever he thinks of the party. He thinks he'll never get it ready in time. And for us to be good servants these days, we have to obey his orders however silly they may be, whether we want to or not. It's a real nuisance to wait on a cranky old man.

JOSSE: The more you try to get things done in a hurry, the less you get them done at all. A lot of good it did me to speak to that scoundrel. I'll give him a good hiding if I get carried away by my anger.

ANTOINE: [*Aside*] Not on your life. All he talks about is giving people a hiding. His wits left him the day he fell in love. He'll kill everyone to get even.

JOSSE: Isn't it enough to infuriate you? Madeleine's probably thinking I won't take the trouble to go and visit her; that's the reason she greeted me so coldly. It's not my fault if I hesitate to visit her. I would go as I am, but Madeleine[63] makes fun of me when she sees me looking like this, wearing so many furs and layers of clothing under my jacket.

ANTOINE: [*Aside*] To tell the truth, these clothes[64] are hardly any better. He wants to dress fashionably without having to pay.

JOSSE: Ah, here comes my servant. Come here, you scoundrel. What keeps me from showing you that you'd better obey your master?

ANTOINE: What do you mean? Do you think that a servant can always manage everything as well as he'd like? In that case one would have to do nothing else.

JOSSE: He still won't keep quiet. —Oh, so I'm the one in the wrong, I see. But you'll learn soon enough how vexed I am.

ANTOINE: Don't you know I can't take a step without meeting either Madeleine or Marion, who make a point of stopping me just to have me tell them how you are. And for this you're always shouting at me.

JOSSE: If that were it, I'd never complain.

ANTOINE: Your humour gets worse every day. Do as you like from now on, but unless you calm down, you'll have a hard time finding a servant who'll put up with you.

JOSSE: You've never seen me stay angry for long. But tell me Antoine, my boy, on your word of honour, did you see them?

ANTOINE: Yes, I did.

JOSSE: Aren't they upset that I didn't go?

ANTOINE: Yes, they are. Madeleine spoke to me about the wedding, and when it would be. I think she wishes it were over with already.

JOSSE: Ah, God! Why am I wasting time here? Come, Antoine, give me that outfit quickly. I'm afraid my father Gérard won't like it if I arrive too late.

ANTOINE: [*Aside*] God knows I was in real danger of getting a good thrashing before I got out of his hands. But I knew how to escape. This is how to hoodwink him and make him think that black is white.[65] [*Exit*]

JOSSE: I see that a mistress can do what she will with her lover. But to tell the truth, I feel happier being loved and being in love.

SCENE IV

GERARD, MARION, JOSSE

GERARD: Here is our gallant, Marion. Do you see how his eye sparkles? How full of vim and vigour he is? How the thought of the feast makes his mouth water! You'd think by looking at him that he'd never want to do it on the sly. But if he found the girl at his feet, can you imagine how eagerly he'd offer his services?

MARION: By Saint John, just as you would.

GERARD: Ah, Marion, I'd better keep still. I'm not up to it any more.

JOSSE: God keep you.

GERARD: And how are you?

JOSSE: As lively as ever.

GERARD: So I see. Tell me, has the first bite given you an appetite?

JOSSE: It's true, little by little I'm managing to get it back.

GERARD: Indeed, so it would seem, since I see you've found what you wanted, and I congratulate you for it. By heaven, I'd have done the same.

MARION: [Aside] I see trouble brewing. Our plot will be found out.

GERARD: You're not saying anything; why the big secret?

JOSSE: What do you mean?

GERARD: Tell me about it, we're alone.

MARION: For heaven's sake, you're pestering him. Do you think he's afraid of someone? Let's forget that and go see Madeleine.

JOSSE: I'd like to know what you're laughing about.

MARION: [Aside] I can't find a way to make them change the subject.

JOSSE: I won't rest until you tell me what this is all about.

MARION: Let's go in. Must I keep telling you?

GERARD: But how does he keep from laughing?

JOSSE: For goodness sake I'm not laughing. What do you mean?

GERARD: All right, I'll say no more. Now that you've done it once, you'll do it even better the second time.

JOSSE: Who says so?

GERARD: I do, I saw you.

JOSSE: I swear you are mistaken and I assure you, father, that I would never wrong Madeleine like that. What's more I'll give fifty crowns to anyone who'll say he saw me commit such gross indecency. I give you my word.

MARION: [Aside] Ah, Marion! Now they'll discover everything.

GERARD: But Master Josse, what's the point of hiding it from me? Do you think I'll spread it around?

JOSSE: Be that as it may, there is not a grain of truth in what you say.

GERARD: Well and good. But tell me what you were doing just now with Madeleine.

JOSSE: What I was doing?

GERARD: Yes, you, I saw you embracing, the two of you, together on the couch in her room.

JOSSE: Upon my word, you're talking nonsense. I haven't set foot in your house today.

GERARD: God above, I'm not raving. I followed you closely enough to hold onto your coat tails.

JOSSE: And you saw me on the couch with her?

GERARD: On my life, I did. Do you think I'm going to deny it? What, isn't that where you were?

JOSSE: I swear you're mistaken. It was someone else, and *I* wash my hands of it. Now that another has moved in, he can marry her. You can be sure I wasn't planning to have his leftovers.

GERARD: What do you mean?

JOSSE: Since someone else had the pleasure of being the first and is so well on the way, he can finish it off. As for me, I thank you for your daughter and I'll ask you please to return the jewels, the gilt chain and the rings that I gave her.

GERARD: I think it is you who got things on the way and no one else, so you should be the one to finish it off.

JOSSE: On my word, I swear somebody else can do what he likes with the creature. And since my mind is made up, I intend to have back what I gave her when the deal was made.

GERARD: Do you think you can get out of it so easily? Is this all that bothers you after what you've done?

JOSSE: She's the one you caught in the act.

GERARD: Yes, but she was with you.

JOSSE: Calm yourself; come to your senses. You'll certainly find it's not so.

GERARD: What's holding me back.

JOSSE: What! Do you expect me to marry a harlot?

GERARD: Liar!

JOSSE: Liar yourself. You're making a liar out of me? On my manhood, you scoundrel, I'll get every cent you have. You old hypocrite with your lying tongue.

GERARD: And you have the audacity to look me in the eye as if I were a blockhead?[66] Are you so transformed since this morning when you put on your new clothes? Ah, if only I were as young and vigorous as I used to be. By heaven, sticks would have to be expensive if I didn't break some on the back of this ruffian.

JOSSE: You're the ruffian, and a skinflint who wants me to marry against my will, and on top of that wants to keep my gold jewels without seeing how impudent you are.

GERARD: You're making me lose patience. I'm coming after you.

JOSSE: Come on then, I'm ready for you. I'm not afraid, you thief, you wretch, you fraud you.

GERARD: I'll tell the police about the wrong you've done to me, you infamous scoundrel! Then everyone will know what's become of your wife. It's only right after you did as you pleased in my house. I can't take any more. You'll soon find out you've met your match in me.

JOSSE: Not on your life, and you'll find that out before the hour is up. [*Exit*]

GERARD: No! I'll have the law on you and see you get the punishment you deserve, or may the Lord strike me dead. Ah, God's mercy, what's holding me back? Oh, he's not going to wait for me. [*Exit*]

MARION: Now's the time to put an end to all of this. Since I've come this far in breaking off the engagement, all that's left are the finishing touches.

SCENE V

MADELEINE, MARION

MADELEINE: Alas, Marion, why is my heart so full of fear? I'm at my wit's end; my courage fails me. My father came rushing in, in a great rage, and I think he suspects something, for instead of greeting me he scowled at me, and forbade me to come near him as though he couldn't stand the sight of me.

MARION: That's better than nothing.

MADELEINE: Tell me, Marion, does he know?

MARION: Yes. The devil with Josse! Whatever I did or said,[67] I couldn't prevent him from finding out almost as much as I know myself.

MADELEINE: Blessed Virgin, what am I to do?

MARION: Come along, child, they'll never catch us. I know what I'm going to do. There's no use crying your heart out.[68]

MADELEINE: But Marion, suppose he were to come into my room. Dear God! How can I stay here? What they say is true: every pleasure brings a thousand sorrows in its wake. Ah me, I'm the unluckiest person that ever loved.

MARION: Don't cry. If the worst comes to the worst, I'll find a way out of this muddle. I've seen some things in my time, and I'm still around. I'll see if I can't salvage my reputation this time as I did in the past.

MADELEINE: If Monsieur[69] knew about this, I'm sure he'd spare nothing for me — not his money, his body, his life, nor his honour, for he is so courageous that he'd sooner die than forsake me.

MARION: Leave everything to me.[70] I'll take care of you as I would of myself.

MADELEINE: But do hurry.

MARION: Don't you worry about anything, just keep your spirits up. You can rest assured so long as I'm out there on the battlefield.

MADELEINE: You're the only one I can count on. I hope, since my need is so great, that you'll protect my honour and my life.

MARION: Haven't I said enough? I want to accomplish something today that will be to my credit.

MADELEINE: I rely on you for everything.

MARION: Be brave. [*Aside*] She won't believe God without a guarantee. —I'll see to everything.

MADELEINE: Heavens, how full love is of sweetness and bitterness and how it poisons the heart. Its taste is both bitter and sweet, it always feeds a poor lover's vain hopes.

SCENE VI

ADVOCATE, JULIEN, GENTLEMAN

ADVOCATE: Julien, I must find a way to speak to my cousin.

JULIEN: Look, I see him. He's coming towards us.

GENTLEMAN: Well, what news?

ADVOCATE: Happiness always wherever I go, and high hopes for the greatest pleasure of them all. And you, cousin?

GENTLEMAN: Just the woman for me. She's a spry filly. No need to spur her to make her run. She can leap a thousand hurdles.

ADVOCATE: Cousin, her grace, her bearing and her dignity deserve everything I can do for love of her.

GENTLEMAN: Cousin, on my word she's the prettiest you'll find and she understands her profession better than any woman in the neighbourhood.

ADVOCATE: I haven't yet been able to kiss her as often as I would like. But if only I can get to her. . . .

GENTLEMAN: She knows how to entertain you, more than I can say.

JULIEN: [*Aside*] Lovers never talk of anything but themselves. If one is all excited the other is no better off. This one talks of his

Madeleine, that one of his new mistress. Heaven knows which
of them is more eager to tell all about his adventure.

ADVOCATE: No, no, cousin, believe me: I am the most fortunate
young lover there is.

GENTLEMAN: I'm to see her again today.

JULIEN: [*Aside*] Which of them is more agitated? Look at them, neither one will keep quiet when the other one talks.

GENTLEMAN: And what about your love affair? Tell me how it's going.

ADVOCATE: By heaven cousin, I've been dying to. I've suffered
more from having to wait so long to tell you than I ever did
from the pangs of love.

GENTLEMAN: Did you get what you wanted?

ADVOCATE: Can you imagine anything else?

GENTLEMAN: I just can't believe it.

ADVOCATE: It's true.

GENTLEMAN: How was it?

ADVOCATE: Do you want the details?

GENTLEMAN: Indeed I do. Come now, tell me how you managed to
make everything go so well.

ADVOCATE: The memory of such heavenly delight is enough to
drive me out of my mind. Here's how it was. Once I got inside
the house, I found myself face to face with my Madeleine. I
leave you to imagine her beauty, the warmth of her embrace,
her words, her smiles and her gracious manner. Then I entered her chamber in anticipation of fulfilment. Marion followed us. As soon as she saw me inside she closed the door.
There I am, and as I am pretty hot-blooded in this kind of
combat, I feel my courage rising.[71] With such good fortune on
my side, I eagerly strip down to my doublet, at which point
Madeleine begins to protest and begs me not to try anything.
Then, as I see tears in her eyes, I feel myself grow more
troubled. The bolder I grow the weaker I find myself. Just the
same, I forge ahead, seeing that the time is ripe, and even
though she is displeased, I turn a blind eye and a deaf ear,
and resolve to take no account of her tears. So to make a long
story short, here I am kissing her and pushing her towards the
foot of the couch. She resists. I press on (first bolting the door
of course), she struggles — but it was just struggling for the
sake of modesty. Love overcame her, love vanquished her and
made her blush. With becoming shame she says, "Love overwhelms me; farewell, pleasures of my youth!" Imagine, cousin,
how marvelous it was.

GENTLEMAN: Yes, for you, brother.

JULIEN: [*Aside*] Julien, my poor friend, wouldn't you be fed up — and restless and out of sorts — if you weren't getting some of it too. No, I'll bet my life our young lover was quick enough to help her get over her fright.[72]

GENTLEMAN: Cousin, let's go to Claude's house. I'll show you my latest conquest.[73]

ADVOCATE: Julien, you wait for Marion to find out what the next step is. [*Exeunt*]

JULIEN: You can be sure that while looking after your interest I won't forget my own if I can get inside the pants of some little wench that suits me. You stripped down to your doublet, but I'll give my shirt to get the woman I have in mind. Listening to him I've become all worked up, and so would any monk, even if his conscience were as great as his learning.

ACT V

SCENE I

PANTALEONE, JULIEN

PANTALEONE: Will my wound be everlasting, since this heartless mistress will give me no relief from my torment? Though she pays no heed to my anguish and my complaining, at least she will hear the sound of my doleful song:

> Ingiustissimo Amor, perché sì raro
> corrispondenti fai nostri desiri?
> onde, perfido, avvien che t'è sì caro
> il discorde voler ch'in duo cor miri?
> Gir non mi lasci al facil guado e chiaro,
> e nel più cieco e maggior fondo tiri:
> da chi disia il mio amor tu mi richiami,
> e chi m'ha in odio vuoi ch'adori ed ami.[74]

JULIEN: Isn't it that scoundrelly rogue I just heard, swaggering along and croaking out his poltroonish poetry? Yes it is, but unless he tunes his rattly instrument a little better, he'll never get what he came for — not if he keeps using that old lute.[75]

PANTALEONE: Come, come my lad: soften the cruelty of this proud woman with your honest service and your ever-so-humble entreaty.

> Fai ch'a Rinaldo Angelica par bella,
> quando esso a lei brutto e spiacevol pare:
> quando le parea bello e l'amava ella,
> egli odiò lei quanto si può odiare.
> Ora s'affligge indarno e si flagella;
> così renduto ben gli è pare a pare;
> ella l'ha in odio, e l'odio è di tal sorte,
> che più tosto che lui vorria la morte.[76]

JULIEN: [*Aside*] Never could such phony talk affect a Frenchman. He doesn't settle for such capers, songs and serenades. That kind of thing can't distract him from what he wants.

PANTALEONE: Ah, cruel one! Will you forever disdain the steadfast love of your most constant servant?

JULIEN: [*Aside*] Call her cruel and be her servant if you like, you'll never win her, Sir Scatterbrain.

PANTALEONE: [*Seeing Julien*] Ah, you wretch!

JULIEN: In agony, are you? Come, Signor mio, give us a song.

PANTALEONE: A beating is what I'd rather give to this lout who plays the braggart.

JULIEN: You're just a bag of wind. I know you. I can tell your kind just by the look of you.

PANTALEONE: God's blood! Does this uncouth yokel think he can make a fool of me? Do you think I'm going to keep quiet?

JULIEN: The first of the house of Frenzy,[77] he's chief squire of the manor — when he's alone.

PANTALEONE: Shall I endure such an affront, I who never quailed in the midst of canon-fire? [*Beats Julien*]

JULIEN: Help! I'm being murdered!

PANTALEONE: I've cut and thrust a thousand times in the thick of battle, and this scurvy knave measures my person against his cowardice.

JULIEN: Do you realize what you're doing, you cur, you Roman spectre, you stinking flea-bag, you gallow's bait, you beggar's scraps. If you don't speak more softly to me I'll beat your brains out. Look at me, I'm Julien, and I don't understand a word of Italian. But if you snarl one more time, I'll make you speak French, you bugger.[78]

PANTALEONE: No, no, messer Juliano, I mistook you for someone else. I'm yours to command. I'd never do anything to displease you.

JULIEN: Yes, and I know who you are only too well. You'll find out soon enough how much I dislike your silly chatter.[79]

SCENE II

JOSSE, ANTOINE, JULIEN, GERARD, PANTALEONE

JOSSE: I'll show them that my courage hasn't failed me.

ANTOINE: Sir, once you've killed him, what am I to do with him?

JOSSE: Whenever I look at this fine armour I have on it reminds me of the defeat at Cerisoles.[80]

ANTOINE: That's where you learned how to kill Italians.

JULIEN: [Aside] It's my lily-livered Italian he's after.

ANTOINE: [Aside] God in heaven. My master's on his last legs and he still talks about beating people over the head.

JOSSE: Antoine, go and order him to return my jewels. If he won't I'll cut him to ribbons and carve him in pieces after he's dead.

ANTOINE: Up and at 'em, sir. I'm on my way.

JOSSE: Have no fear. With this halbert I'll be like an advance squadron, for I've seen a good bit of war in my time.

JULIEN: [Aside] To listen to him thunder, you'd think it was about to rain.

GERARD: [Enters and notices Josse] So here you are. I'm in the mood to give you a taste of my sword.

ANTOINE: Ah, sir, here he comes.

JOSSE: Stand fast, Antoine, don't run away. I'll just keep a few paces behind to help in case he's brought anyone to catch us off guard.

GERARD: Since this is what he wants, I'll show him that I'm man enough. I can make a stand as stout and spirited as his attack.

JOSSE: Come on, to his door. Let's go inside — break it down!

GERARD: Before you do, you'll find out what kind of man I am.

PANTALEONE: Ah, gentlemen, gentlemen, be patient! Show greater forbearance. Messer Gérard, restrain yourself.

GERARD: Ah, if I let my bravery carry me away, I'll teach you not to be so insolent.

JOSSE: By Jove, I'm not afraid of you.

GERARD: I dare you to take another step. You're not too big for me to take a stick to you.

JOSSE: Great boasters, small roasters.

JULIEN: Gentlemen, shall I tell you what happened? All this trouble and commotion is the Italian's doing. I just saw him leaving your house. No sooner was he out than he ran away to change his clothes. In fact, he used all his strength to take your daughter by force. But he didn't succeed. If you don't believe me, he told me himself. Would I lie to you? Now that he's all worked up, he keeps coming back, just to begin the same thing over again.

GERARD: Come, neighbour, help me to catch this hypocrite, this scoundrel, this lecher.

JOSSE: And you were so sure I was the one.

PANTALEONE: Hey, there, watch what you're doing! Wait a minute, what is this?

JOSSE: A poke in the ribs.

JULIEN: Wait, I have other witnesses. I'll go call them. Meanwhile, hold on to him.

JOSSE: You knave, you traitor, you scoundrel! You thought you'd corrupt my wife.

GERARD: I wondered why he kept coming here.

PANTALEONE: But gentlemen, I've done nothing!

JOSSE: No, father, we'll hold him fast. I'll wait here all day if I have to.

SCENE III

GENTLEMAN, AGNES, JULIEN, ADVOCATE

GENTLEMAN: Madame, I assure you that you can trust me entirely. I will always have fifty crowns to show my love for you and protect your rights.

AGNES: Indeed I don't deserve so great an honour. But I give you my word, sir, that as long as I live I will remember you and will be ready to render you any service I can.

GENTLEMAN: Believe me, if there is justice in this city[81] it will be done.

AGNES: Indeed, that's all I wish for.

GENTLEMAN: After that, you can easily make me happy.

AGNES: Sir, you know I am ready to do whatever I can.

JULIEN: [*Entering*] Now's our chance to launch an attack. Not only that, we can advance.

ADVOCATE: You must be joking.

JULIEN: Joking, Sir? Not on your life. I've just left some pretty astonished people. [*Whispers*]

GENTLEMAN: They're certainly in for a fall, Josse as much as the Italian. Now we know how to get what we want.

JULIEN: If ever I needed my wits about me, now's the time. They won't catch me off guard.

ADVOCATE: You're a friend in need. Please, cousin, let's hurry up.

GENTLEMAN: We don't need you here. Leave everything to me. Off you go.

ADVOCATE: If you insist. But please, if my life means anything to you. . . .

GENTLEMAN: Still not convinced? Julien, come with me.

JULIEN: The Italian has been arrested in your place, and has already been quarrelling with Gérard for quite a while.

GENTLEMAN: He'll never get her, he's finished.

ADVOCATE: And how will I learn what all this squabbling has come to?

JULIEN: Don't worry. I won't leave out a thing.

ADVOCATE: But listen to me. Where Madeleine's concerned, I'm putting myself in your hands.

GENTLEMAN: That's a lover for you! He's so fearful and full of doubt that he can't see what's in front of him.

JULIEN: My master is so madly in love that he won't believe God without a guarantee.

GENTLEMAN: Let's go, Madame Agnès.

JULIEN: [Aside] She's a professional. I can tell just by looking at her heels.[82]

AGNES: Sir, I trust you with my honour.

SCENE IV

GERARD, JOSSE, PANTALEONE, AGNES, GENTLEMAN, JULIEN

GERARD: Hang on there, here are the ones who claim you tried to seduce her.

JOSSE: By God, I'll haul you up before the courts.

PANTALEONE: Hear me first.

JOSSE: No, even if it costs me my last penny, now that we've found you out I'll make you pay dearly for your wickedness. Don't let go, father Gérard.

AGNES: [To Gentleman] Sir, do you see that old man who is shouting and straining to hold onto that man?[83] It's Josse, my husband.

GENTLEMAN: I'd already noticed him; I thought I recognized him.

JULIEN: [Aside] Now I'll introduce them to each other. Come, Madame Agnès; this way, sir.

JOSSE: Holy Virgin, I just had the fright of my life. By heaven, I thought I'd breathed my last. It looked like my wife. It is my wife.

GERARD: What's the matter with you? You've suddenly changed colour.

GENTLEMAN: He doesn't know which way to turn with all this to-do, so it's no wonder he's not his usual self. But hear me, Master Josse, come over here. Do you recognize her?

PANTALEONE: Leave that woman alone, she belongs to me.

GENTLEMAN: Ah you dog, why don't I crack your skull?

PANTALEONE: By heaven, she's mine.

GENTLEMAN: Out of my sight or hold your tongue, or I swear I'll make your head roll. What, haven't you had enough?

PANTALEONE: I ask for the protection of the King. Is this a country where force rules over justice?

GENTLEMAN: God's life! Do you suppose anybody cares what you think?

JOSSE: And it all comes back to land on me, for I can see very well everyone has had his fill,[84] while I, poor wretch, will get the leftovers.

PANTALEONE: Sir, give up your claim to her; once you hear me out, I'm sure you won't want to hold her back, and I think that if you had taken as many pains for her as I have. . . .

JULIEN: [Aside] If she were beautiful there'd be murder to pay for sure. But in fact all the beauty I see wouldn't get a rise out of me.[85]

GENTLEMAN: I can't get over you, you pack of degenerates! Do you think you can overwhelm us with your lying tongue, as though our own downtrodden language couldn't say a single word in reply? Do you think French is so gross that it is less expressive than your silly and effeminate tongue which, like thick smoke, overwhelms us at first and ends by blowing away with the wind? Our France is fed up with your tricks and chicanery.[86]

PANTALEONE: I maintained her in Lyons for three years, and went to great trouble and expense to bring her to this city.

JULIEN: [Aside] And she's had fifty thousand lovers in the meantime: she's done it with weak ones and strong ones. Just think of such an appetite — taking on anyone, big or small, for they say that in the game of making love, a change only sharpens the desire to re-enter the fray and rekindle the flames of love.

GERARD: Well neighbour? Is this worthy of a man of honour? For one thing, you see your wife is still alive; she's ready for you and wants to come back home, and here you are trying to marry someone else. Since the law forbids the dissolution of these holy bonds, you tried to trick me. But watch out, I'll spend all I have to see such villainy punished.

AGNES: I'll have the law on you. And I'll make you carry two distaffs,[87] so that all the world can see your crime.

JULIEN: [Aside] Say, that's not bad. She tells him off, before he can get a word in. Now that's the way to come home when you're feeling guilty.

JOSSE: Away with you, you vile creature. First with a scoundrel, then with an Italian; in fact you lifted up your skirts[88] to anyone who came along, no matter that they were strangers, no matter that you didn't know them, even to stable-boys and tramps. And now you want to come home to me.

AGNES: What's a woman supposed to do with you? You get feebler by the day. A lot of good you'll do me!

JULIEN: [*Aside*] What he needs is a lackey like me to help him out.[89] I'll make up for the time he's lost and do what he can't do any more.

JOSSE: And what about me? I would rather die than put up with the wrong that this creature has done me.

GENTLEMAN: By God, I'll tell the police what he's been up to.

GERARD: There's nothing I wouldn't do to avoid a scandal.

AGNES: No, no. Believe me, I'll have you pilloried in the public square for wanting to marry two women.

JOSSE: Gentlemen, you see how she insults me? You're all witnesses.

AGNES: Just let me get my hands on you, you wretch. . . .

JULIEN: [*Aside*] What a devil she is. With one look at her, you can tell she's the mistress. Believe me, I'm not surprised she sold herself.

GERARD: Do you want to know what I think, neighbour? Look what a predicament you're in, and it's to the honour and advantage of both of you to get out of it. After all, she's your wife. You know, we've only one soul to save or lose. No matter how far we go astray, we always have to come back. It's futile to persist in hatred and rancour. Her honour should be yours, and your fortune hers. Since, by God's grace, you've lived until today, let's have an end to this quarrel that has caused you such grief. The goat must browse where she is tied.

JOSSE: What do you mean? Can I live with a woman who has so wronged me? I'd rather die.

GENTLEMAN: Think of your dishonour if this disgrace were to come to the attention of the authorities.

JOSSE: Very well. I will make peace if Agnès promises never to go back there.

GENTLEMAN: And so she will.

AGNES: I will, but at the same time he must promise not to scold me so much any more.

JOSSE: By St. James, I agree. Here's my hand.

AGNES: There, that's settled.

JOSSE: I thank you heartily, Sir, for all you've done.

GERARD: I'd still like to know who's going to repay me.[90]

GENTLEMAN: Come now, Madame Agnès, be nice to Monsieur Josse.

AGNÈS: Indeed sir, I'll do the best I can.[91]

PANTALEONE: And what about me?

GENTLEMAN: Be quiet or you'll get the drubbing you deserve. Don't you know the money she spent was her husband's?

GERARD: Quick, a constable to take this knave into custody. He disguised himself as Master Josse and did everything he could to take Madeleine by force.[92] Ho there, you servants. Come here, the lot of you.

GENTLEMAN: You see how things are. Get out of here before you get into trouble.

GERARD: Seize him.

PANTALEONE: You'll never catch hold of me, you and all your fine constables. [*Runs off*]

GENTLEMAN: Master Gérard, let's go in, and I'll tell you the whole story.

GERARD: I can't get over that wretch. I swear if I ever find him. . . .

GENTLEMAN: Julien, go bring my cousin while I wait here.

JULIEN: I will.

GERARD: And you, neighbour, what about the other business?

JOSSE: I'll go along with whatever you wish.

GERARD: Agreed. [*Exeunt*]

JULIEN: Whew! Now our young lover will jump for joy. Wait till he hears how cleverly I managed everything. I can see him now, overjoyed, laughing and leaping, playing and dancing in the midst of the celebration, and suddenly embracing me as the cause of his happiness. When I think how thrilled he'll be with the news I'm bringing him, my heart leaps in my breast. He's won his Cruel Lady at last, and his heart will yearn no more. This is his reward for his long constancy.

And you, gentlemen, who don't regret the time we spent talking of this wanton love — if ardour has enflamed your heart, or if hope now reopens your wound, stand firm. I'm sure such a love will make you even happier than my master. And if you can't manage it on your own, Julien will always be more than happy to oblige you too. Meanwhile, take my word for it, there's no time to lose.

NOTES

1 "Faisans Mercure/De chasque bois mal raboté" in the French text. The meaning is obscure. According to Randle Cotgrave, *A Dictionarie of the French and English Tongues* (London, 1611), "Il a du mercure à la teste" means "He is fantasticall, humorous, new-fangled, giddie-headed; also, he is verie craftie." The sense may be that the nitwits ("estourdis") put on outlandish performances wherever they can find a rough-hewn plank to turn into a stage in order to please ("servir") the University.

2 The passage is obscure. Grévin appears to be referring to the medieval plays, which he despises. The reference to the University is not clear. Certainly the University was a bastion of conservatism under the control of the Church and therefore distasteful to Grévin as a humanist and Protestant. Raymond Lebègue, "La Tragédie 'shakespearienne' en France au temps de Shakespeare," in *Études sur le théâtre français* (Paris, 1977), 304, believes that Grévin is associating the University with bombastic performances of early blood-and-thunder Senecan plays.

3 Possibly they are the Italian actors who, though they first appeared at the court of Henri III in 1577, are known to have given public performances as early as 1548, though there is no evidence of their association with the University in Grévin's day. The upstart actors are in the text "nouveaux basteleurs," translated by Cotgrave as "A iugler, tumbler, puppet-player." The "farcical tragedies and moralizing farces" is a contemptuous reference to the blend of morality and farce in medieval plays. These did not adhere to Aristotelian precepts and Grévin accordingly speaks of them disparagingly. In the Prologue to *La Trésorière* Grévin also objects to the mingling of the sacred and the profane on the stage.

4 An apparent pun. The French text, "gros mots qu'on ne peult entendre," refers to the coarseness of the speech and action in the earlier theatre. "Entendre" can also be taken to mean "understand": there would thus be a slighting reference to the Italian language which is both offensive and incomprehensible. Grévin's objection would therefore be on moral, linguistic, aesthetic and nationalistic grounds.

5 Possibly a reference to the *Poetics*, Chapter 14. In *BD*, 6 Grévin refers to Aristotle, but nowhere to the concept of catharsis.

6 The Place Maubert is just beyond the Mont-Sainte-Geneviève, the seat of the University of Paris. Traditionally a meeting place of scholars, it was, and is, a solid middle-class district. The action of Grévin's first comedy, *La Trésorière*, takes place in the vicinity of the Place Maubert and its portrait of Constante, the adulterous heroine, may have offended women in the audience.

7 Close to the Place Maubert. By the end of the 11th century, St. Séverin served as a parish church for the whole of the left bank. The present church was begun as early as the 13th century, with construction and renovation continuing until 1530.

8 "Ils parlent d'encherir le pain" in the French text: they talk about the price of bread; i.e., of trivial matters.

9 "Ce beau train," which we translate as "galavanting," has, according to Lapeyre, a conspiratorial connotation. The expression "Laisser atteindre le chat au fromage" in the original: a coarse expression referring to an unchaste woman.

10 Josse is here referring to the Gascon whom Claude describes in III.ii.

11 The French text uses the expression "Avoir fer qui loche": to complain about something (originally referring to a horse whose shoe is loose).

12 Antwerp edition variant: which will be mine on my wedding day.

13 Marion says literally that one must cover one's rear guard (as in a military manoeuvre).

14 "C'est la toux du renard", a deep-seated and rasping cough, in the French text. When Marion calls it "The best thing there is about you," she is of course being sarcastic.

15 Antwerp variant: too much.

16 Literally, "My tool (member) is every bit as lively as yours is."

17 In the French text, "Vous estes de ces grans parleurs,/ Et aussi des petis faiseurs:/Vous estes trop beau pour bien mordre." That is: You're a brave talker, but a poor performer. You're too nice to bite.

18 The state of the hand was generally considered in the Renaissance to be a sign of one's amorous condition. Cf. *Othello* III.iv, where the hero believes Desdemona's hot and moist hand betrays a lecherous heart.

19 In the French text, "Qui bon l'achette, bon le boit" (proverb). Literally: he who pays well drinks well.

20 The many-headed hydra at Lerna which so devastated the land that it was sought out and slain by Hercules with the aid of Iolaus (the second of his twelve labours). Antwerp variant: this mop good only to sweep out a cistern.

21 The French text reads, "Il semble à veoir à vieille vache/Qu'oncques genise ne besa." Evidently a proverbial expression whose meaning is obscure. Literally: "You'd think, seeing the (an?) old cow that as a heifer it had never kissed"; or: "Seeing the old cow, you'd swear that as a heifer it never made love." Even the syntax is not clear, as "genise" (heifer) could be either the subject or the object of the verb "besa" (baisa: kissed or made love). "Beser" in Old French also has the meaning: to go wild, speaking of a cow stung by gadflies. The two verbs, while they can be spelled alike, do not have the same derivation.

22 The round cap was worn by men of law.

23 I.e., Madeleine.

24 Antwerp variant: to deceive the first man.

25 Antwerp variant: I delight in my torment, being constrained and coerced by her great beauty.

26 The original reads, "Si en trouve l'on d'aussi belles": One can find others equally fine.

27 "Car si bien luy sceut attacher/A gros clous d'amour sa pensée" in the French text: She has so thoroughly fixed his thoughts on her with nails of love.

28 The translation is an exact rendering of the original mixed metaphor.

29 In the Antwerp edition, Julien's speech ends with "be useful to such a fine master" and the Advocate's begins, "And I give you my word Julien. . . ."

30 "Il a disné d'une salade,/Et au dessert d'une gambade" in the original. Our translation fails to convey the pun on "salade" which in addition to its modern meaning, denotes a helmet or headpiece.

31 "Trainer ses dandrilles" in the French text: Dragging his gonads.

32 Ariosto, *Orlando Furioso*, 2 vols., ed. Emilio Bigi (Milan, 1982), XXXV, 2:

> But to regain my sanity, I know
> I have no need to journey to the moon
> Or to the realms of Paradise to go,
> For not so high my scattered wits have flown.
> Your eyes, your brow, your breasts as white as snow,
> Your limbs detain them here, and I will soon
> Retrace them with my lips where'er they went,
> And gather them once more, with your consent.

Translated by Barbara Reynolds, 2 Vols. (Harmondsworth, 1977), Vol. II, 336. Reprinted by permission of Penguin Books Ltd.

33 The "sidekicks" of St. Anthony ("Toni" in the text) are swine, and the "disease of St. Lazarus" is leprosy. The text is in macaronic French.

34 I.e., Antoine.

35 Antwerp variant: moping at the thought of this wedding.

36 Antoine again: cf. the following scene.

37 Arrangement. A variant on "mesnage" (household) in the 1561 edition is "message." Our translation accommodates both texts.

38 The French text reads, "Sous l'ombre d'un boisseau de pois." According to Lapeyre, the expression "a bushel of peas" conveys the irony of enclosing something trifling in a container of large capacity.

39 "Ces paieurs en gambades" in the original: Cotgrave: "payer en gambades," "to runne away when he should pay."

40 In the French, "Sans beste vendre": without loss or injury.

41 Another obscure passage which seems to mean, literally: "And where they want to undertake it, I leave it up to the malcontents." "Entreprendre": undertake, may here be used as a noun with a licentious connotation. The malcontents are, presumably, dissatisfied customers.

42 "Une religieuse/Du bas mestier" in the original: i.e., a common prostitute, commonly called a nun in the 16th century. In the next line a brothel is called a convent.

43 "Tous les marchans de l'ordinaire" in the French text: Tavern keepers, according to Cotgrave.

44 Pinvert edition: every evening brings its bread.

45 Antwerp variant: as long as I'm still alive.

46 The "girl" turns out to be Dame Agnès, already referred to. She does not appear until V.iii.

47 On August 9, 1557, the French army was defeated at Saint-Quentin, after a lengthy siege, by the Spanish. To commemorate the victory, Philip II constructed the Escurial north of Madrid.

48 Lyons was throughout the 16th century the second most important cultural centre in France. It was also on the trade route from Paris to south-eastern France and Italy and was therefore the chief centre through which Italian goods and ideas passed on their way northward.

49 The original contains two colloquial expressions: "Luy coupant la queue tout court," to cut someone's tail short, meaning to abandon someone; and "De son eau beniste de court," with his holy water of the court, meaning flattery or false promises.

50 The young Italian is Pantaleone.

51 Zeus, in the likeness of Amphitryon, her husband, seduced Alcmena. From this union Hercules was born.

52 Antwerp variant: a lover.

53 Antwerp variant: loosen.

54 I.e., Antoine.

55 In the original edition this line does not rhyme with any other. In the Antwerp version of the 1562 edition, Grévin pads out the line thus: "There is no quarrel between them which, it seems to me, has not in this way. . . ."

56 Antwerp variant: I want her to bring honour to me as a child should her father.

57 Antwerp variant: Had I not wanted her to come round of her own accord, my mind would by now have been at rest. For I want her to marry. However, to marry in haste. . . .

58 According to Lapeyre, p. 164, this soliloquy is in the tradition of what, in the 17th century, became known as the *jouissance*, a celebration of sexual pleasure.

59 The Antwerp edition deletes the last line of Scene i ("While my heart beats strong").

60 The Antwerp edition adds: "Since you've begun the wedding. . . ."

61 Antwerp variant: I do believe that Josse has recently grown a good ten years younger.

62 The original reads, ". . . il ne peult attendre/Sans sur la fournée entreprendre." The expression means to do something ahead of time out of impatience. Cotgrave translates "Prendre un pain sur la fournée" as "To get a snatch at his wench before she be maryed."

63 Antwerp variant: Marion.

64 I.e., Josse's borrowed cloak that the Advocate has been wearing.

65 In the French text, "Et luy monstrer qu'une vessie/Est une lanterne." A proverbial expression meaning to think or make someone think "the moon is made of green cheese."

66 Literally: And do you have the audacity to raise up your head against me as if I were a dumb animal?

67 Antwerp variant: The devil with him! Clever as I was, I couldn't. . . .

68 "Il n'en fault point crier le ventre" in the French text: You must not complain (from the depths) of your belly.

69 "Monsieur": the Advocate.

70 The French reads, "Laissez faire à Georges, il est homme/d'aage." The original saying appears to have been: Laissez faire à Dieu qui est homme d'âge; that is, leave it to God who is old (and wise). This was modified at the time of Georges d'Amboise, minister under Louis XII, to mean that in a tricky political situation, the minister was the man to turn to. Leroux de Lincy, *Le livre des proverbes français*, 1859 (Rpt. Geneva, 1968).

71 "Je commence à lever la teste" in the original. Cotgrave translates "la teste levée" as boldly, confidently, but the context surely suggests a sexual pun.

72 The original employs the expression "affranchir du loup-garou": to free from the werewolf; i.e., to free from fear.

73 "Tendron" in the original. The gentleman is referring to Dame Agnès, Josse's wife.

74 Ariosto, *Orlando Furioso*, II, 1:

Ah, cruel Love! What is the reason why
You seldom make our longings correspond?
How is it, traitor, you rejoice to spy
Two hearts discordant, one repelled, one fond?
Into the darkest, blindest depths must I
Be drawn, when I might ford a limpid pond?
Towards her who loves, you stifle my desire:
For her who hates, you set my heart on fire.

Translated by Barbara Reynolds. Op. cit., Vol. I, 138. Reprinted by permission of Penguin Books Ltd.

75 Undoubtedly a play on words. The comparison between the sexual member and a musical instrument is common in the Middle Ages and Renaissance.

76 Ariosto, *Orlando Furioso*, II, 2:

You make Rinaldo love Angelica,
While he is ugly in her eyes; and yet
When he seemed handsome and was loved by her,
He hated her, as much as man can hate.
Now in vain torment and desire for her
He suffers retribution, tit for tat.
She hates him and so fierce a hate he stirs
That death to his devotion she prefers.

Translated by Barbara Reynolds. Op. cit., Vol. I, 138. Reprinted by permission of Penguin Books Ltd.

77 "La caze Frenese" in the French text: the house of the Farnesi. Julien deforms the name of one of the most illustrious of Italian families. It was the family name of the dukes of Parma. Pope Paul III (1534-49) was a Farnese. The Farnese palace is now the site of the French embassy in Rome.

78 Julien uses the word "bougrino": known in the 16th century as "le vice italien," later as "le vice anglais."

79 In the original, "sot langage." There is a double meaning, not only idle chatter but also contemptible language — a disdainful reference to Italian.

80 Cerisoles: town in Piedmont in Italy where, in 1544, the French defeated the Spanish. The allusion clearly dates Josse and makes him more ridiculous.

81 Antwerp variant: Paris.

82 A common ribald jest: the courtesan's heels are up in the air.

83 Antwerp variant: that old man who is trying to put up an armed resistance.

84 The expression "Faire ses choux gras" in the French text: to profit from something, to turn it to one's advantage.

85 The French text reads, "Ne peult faire dresser l'oreille/A mon courtault": wouldn't make my horse twitch his ear.

86 For this anti-Italian tirade, see Introduction, p. 15.

87 I.e., show you to be a bigamist. Perhaps also a cuckold, since two sticks suggest horns.

88 The French expression used is "Jouer des mannequins": make love.

89 The French text reads, "Il luy faudroit quelque nacquet/Comme moy, pour le nacqueter/Dedans son jeu." "Nacquet": lackey, valet; "Nacqueter": according to Cotgrave, "To serve (or stop) a ball at Tennis; also, to wait at a great mans doore; (and thence) also, to observe dutifully."

90 Antwerp variant: I'll have to decide what to do.

91 The Antwerp edition omits the interchange between the Gentleman and Agnès.

92 Sentence omitted in the Antwerp edition.